ALMOST
TRANSPARENT
BLUE

ALMOST TRANSPARENT BLUE

Ryu Murakami

Translated by Nancy Andrew

KODANSHA INTERNATIONAL
Tokyo · New York · London

First published in Japanese as *Kagirinaku tōmei ni chikai burū* by Kodansha Ltd., Tokyo, 1976.

Distributed in the United States by Kodansha America, Inc., and in the United Kingdom and continental Europe by Kodansha Europe Ltd.

Published by Kodansha International Ltd., 17-14, Otowa 1-chome, Bunkyo-ku, Tokyo 112-8652, and by Kodansha America, Inc.

ISBN-13: 978-4-7700-2904-1
ISBN-10: 4-7700-2904-7

First edition, 1977
First paperback edition, 1981
First trade paperback edition, 2003
12 11 10 09 08 07 06   12 11 10 9 8 7 6 5

www.kodansha-intl.com

It wasn't the sound of an airplane. The buzz was an insect somewhere behind my ear. Smaller than a fly, it circled for a moment before my eyes, then disappeared into a dark corner of the room.

On the round white tabletop reflecting the ceiling light was an ashtray made of glass. A long, thin, lipstick-smeared cigarette smoldered in it. Near the edge of the table stood a pear-shaped wine bottle, with a picture on its label of a blonde woman, her mouth full of grapes from the bunch she held in her hand. Red light from the ceiling trembled on the surface of the wine in a glass. The ends of the table legs disappeared into the thick pile of the rug. Opposite me was a large dressing table. The back of the woman sitting at it was moist with sweat. She stretched out her leg and rolled off a black stocking.

"Hey, bring me that towel. The pink one, O.K.?" Lilly said, tossing the rolled-up stocking at me. She said she'd just got back from work, picked up the cologne, and lightly patted it on her forehead, which was shiny with grease.

"So then what happened?" she asked, wiping her back with the towel as she looked at me.

"Aw, you know, I thought I'd give him some booze, it might cool him down, and besides him there were two other guys in a car outside, everybody high on glue, you know, so I thought I'd give him some booze. Was he really locked up in the juvie pen?"

"He's a Korean, that guy."

Lilly was taking off her makeup. She wiped her face with a little cotton wad, flattened and soaked with a piercingly fragrant liquid. She leaned over to peer into the mirror and took off her false eyelashes; they were like the fins of a tropical fish. The cotton she tossed away was smeared with red and black.

"Ken, he stabbed his brother, I think maybe it was his brother, but he didn't die, and he came to the bar a little while back."

I gazed through the wine glass at the light bulb. Inside the smooth glass sphere the filament was a dark orange.

"He said he'd asked you about me, Lilly, so watch your mouth, O.K.? Don't tell too much to weird guys like that."

Lilly finished the wine that had been set down among the lipsticks and brushes and various bottles and boxes on the dressing table, then right there in front of me she slipped off her gold lamé slacks. The elastic left a line on her stomach. They said Lilly had done fashion modeling, once.

On the wall hung a framed photo of her in a fur coat. She told me it was chinchilla and cost I don't know how many thousands. One time, when it was cold, she'd come to my room, her face pale as a corpse; she'd shot up too much Philopon. With a rash around her mouth, shaking violently, she'd fallen in as soon as she'd opened the door.

Hey, will you take off my nail polish, it's all sticky and nasty. I'm sure she said something like that as I hugged and lifted her. That time she was wearing a backless dress and was so drenched with sweat that even her pearl necklace was slippery. As I'd wiped her fingernails and toenails clean with paint thinner, since there hadn't been any polish remover, she'd said in a low voice, Sorry, there was something kind of rough at work. While I was holding her ankle and rubbing her toenails, Lilly just stared out the window, breathing deeply. I slipped my hand under the hem of her dress and felt the cold sweat on the inside of her thighs as I kissed her and slid her panties down. With the panties tangled around one foot and her legs spread wide on the chair, Lilly said then, I'd like to watch TV, you know, there should be some old flick with Marlon Brando, some Elia Kazan. The flower-scented sweat on my palms had taken a long time to dry.

"Ryū, you shot up on morphine at Jackson's house, right? Day before yesterday." Lilly was peeling a peach she'd taken out of the refrigerator. Legs crossed, she was sunk deep in the sofa. I waved aside her offer of the peach. "Well, don't you remember a girl there, red dye-job, short skirt, good style, good ass?"

"I don't know, there were three Japanese girls there, you mean the one with the Afro hairdo?"

I could see into the kitchen from where I sat. A black bug, maybe a cockroach, was crawling around on the dirty dishes piled in the sink. Lilly talked on as she wiped peach juice off her bare thighs. She dangled a slipper from one foot, in which I could see the red and blue blood vessels. I always think these are lovely, seen through the skin.

"So she was lying, that bitch, she cut work, said she was sick but she was playing around all day with guys like you—No thanks! Did she shoot up, too?"

"Jackson wouldn't let her do that, would he? It's really a bummer, the way he says girls shouldn't shoot up. So she was from your place, huh? She sure laughed a lot, smoked too much grass and laughed a lot."

"You think she should get fired?"

"But she draws them in, right?"

"Yeah, well, with that kind of ass."

The cockroach had stuck its head on a dish covered with globs of ketchup; its back was shiny with grease.

When you smash cockroaches, the juice comes out in different colors. Maybe the belly of this one was full of red now.

Once, when I killed a roach crawling on a paint palette, the juice was a bright fresh purple. Since there'd been no purple paint on the palette, I thought red and blue must have mixed together in that little belly.

"So what happened about Ken? Did he go home all right?"

"Aw, I let him in and said there're no girls, will you have some booze, but he said sorry, make it a coke, I'm high already. He actually apologized."

"Really dumb, huh?"

"The guys waiting in the car picked up a chick who was just passing by, she was pretty ripe."

What makeup there was left on Lilly's cheeks shone faintly. She tossed the stone of the peach into the ashtray, pulled out the pins to take down her dyed hair, and began to slowly brush its waves, a cigarette drooping from the corner of her mouth.

"Ken's sister used to work at my place, a long time ago, she was pretty smart."

"She quit?"

"Seems she went back to the country, said her home was somewhere up north."

Her soft red hair clung to the brush. After straightening the rich mass of hair, she got up as if she'd just remembered something and took a silver box containing a slender syringe out of the cabinet. She held a small brown bottle up to the light to see how much was inside, drew just the right amount of liquid up into the syringe, and leaned over to shoot it into her thigh. Her other leg trembled slightly. I suppose she put the needle in too deep, because when she took it out, a thin trickle of blood ran down to around the knee. Lilly massaged her temples and wiped away the saliva that had dribbled from the corner of her lips.

"Lilly, you've got to sterilize that needle every time."

Without answering, she lay down on the bed in one corner of the room and lit a cigarette. The thick blood vessels in her neck moved as she puffed out the smoke weakly.

"You want to shoot up, Ryū? There's still some left."

"Not today, I've got some at my place too, and some friends are coming over."

Lilly reached over to the bedside table, picked up a paperback copy of *The Charterhouse of Parma*, and started reading. As she blew smoke on the open page, she seemed to chase after the words with a peaceful absentminded expression.

"Your sure read at weird times, silly Lilly," I said, picking up the syringe that had fallen from the shelf and rolled along the floor. She said, "Yeah, this is good," in a voice that got tangled up in her tongue.

There was blood on the end of the syringe. When I went into the kitchen to wash it off, the cockroach was still working on the dishes in the sink. I rolled up a newspaper and, careful not to break the plates, smashed it after it moved onto the small table by the sink.

"What're you doing?" Lilly asked, scraping the blood from her thigh with her fingernail. "Hey, come over here." Her voice was very sweet.

The juice from the roach was yellow. Smashed on the edge of the table, it stuck there, the antennae still stirring slightly.

Lilly slid off her panties, called me again. *The Charterhouse of Parma* had been tossed on the rug.

A sharp odor filled my room, the smell of an old pineapple on the table. I couldn't remember when I'd cut it. The cut end had gone black, completely rotten, and the syrupy juice lay congealed on the plate.

As Okinawa got ready to shoot up, the tip of his nose glistened with sweat. Seeing that, I thought it really was a hot sticky night, just like Lilly had said. As she'd rocked her body—which must have been growing heavy—on the damp bed, she'd kept saying Hey, aren't you hot, today's really hot.

"Hey, Ryū, how much was that smack?" Reiko asked as she took a record by The Doors out of a leather bag. When I answered $10, Okinawa said loudly, "Oh wow, that's cheaper than back in Okinawa." He was heating the needle of a syringe with a lighter. After sterilizing it with a hunk of cotton soaked in alcohol, he blew on it a couple of times to make sure that the hole wasn't blocked.

"You know, I was really freaked out to see how the walls and the john and stuff had been fixed up, over there at the lockup in Yotsuya, you know, and this young guard bastard was a real blabmouth, right? And he kept making dumb jokes like saying, this is better than the police dorm, and some old guy played along with him by laughing real loud, so I felt really down."

Okinawa's eyes were a muddy yellow. He was drinking odd-smelling liquor from a milk bottle, and he was already pretty drunk when he got to my room.

"Hey, were you really in a drug rehab center back there?"

I asked Okinawa as I opened the aluminum foil with the heroin in it.

"Yeah, my old man put me in, a good ol' Yank-run drug center, since the guy who'd busted me was an M.P., right? First they put me in that G.I. place and had me take a cure, then sent me back here. Hey, Ryū, America's really, you know, advanced, I really thought so."

Reiko, who'd been looking at The Doors' record jacket, cut in, "Yeah, Ryū, don't you think it'd be great to get shot up on morphine every day? I'd like to get into some Yank drug center, too."

Scraping together the heroin from the edges of the foil with an earpick, Okinawa said, "Shit, I told you, small-time users like you can't get in; they only let in real junkies like me, right? Nobody but real addicts—needle marks on both arms, right? There was this nurse there called Yoshiko, kind of sexy, you know, and I got shot up in the butt by her every day. I'd stick out my butt, like this, see? And while I'd be looking out the window at everybody outside, they're playing volleyball or something, she'd shove it to me right in the ass, right? But I was so wasted my cock was all shriveled up and I didn't want Yoshiko baby to see it. A big butt like yours, Reiko, just couldn't make it in there."

Reiko went humph in annoyance, said she wanted something to drink, went into the kitchen and opened the refrigerator.

"Isn't there a-anything?"

Okinawa pointed to the pineapple on the table and said, "Have some of this, it tastes just like home, right?"

"Okinawa, you sure do love rotten things, don't you? What about those clothes, huh? They stink!" Reiko said as she drank some watered-down Calpis, moving an ice cube around in her cheek.

"I'm going to be a junkie real soon, too. I'll just get worn out if I'm not as much of an addict as Okinawa after we get married, and so after we're both hooked we'll live together, right? And then I'd like us to go off it bit by bit.''

"You'd have your honeymoon in a drug center?" I laughed.

"Hey, Okinawa, that's what we'll do, O.K.?"

"That's cool, that's what you should do, you could line up your butts together, real nice, and get shot up with morphine while saying I love you to each other, right?"

Okinawa laughed a little, said, "Shit, stop putting me on," and with a napkin dried off the spoon he'd been soaking in hot water.

With the earprick, he placed a bit of heroin just about the size of a match head in the center of the bow-handled, stainless-steel spoon. "Hey, Reiko, you sneeze or something now and I'll stomp you, you understand?" He fixed the needle in place in a one-cc battlefield syringe. Reiko lit a candle. Using the syringe, he carefully dripped water on the heroin.

"Hey, Ryū, you going to fix up another party?" Okinawa asked, rubbing his slightly shaky fingers on his pants to steady them.

"Yeah, well, those black guys asked me to."

"And you're going, Reiko? To the party, right?" Okinawa asked.

She folded up the rest of the heroin in the foil. Looking at me, she answered, "Yeah, but it's nothing to get uptight about."

"Look, I don't want you to get stoned and screw some black, O.K.?"

He held the spoon over the candle. All of a sudden the solution was boiling. Froth and steam rose from inside the spoon, the bottom was dirty with black soot. Okinawa slowly moved it away from the flame and blew on it to cool it, just like you do when you're going to feed soup to a baby.

"In the clink, you know," he began as he started tearing up a cotton wad. "In the clink, you know, I was going cold turkey, right? Had these nightmares, you know, I don't remember them too well, but I saw my big brother—I'm the fourth son in my family, he was the oldest—I never got to know him, he died fighting in Oroku, there wasn't even a photo of him, just a bad picture my old man had drawn and stuck in the family altar, but anyway there was my big brother in my dreams—wasn't that weird? Wasn't that really far out?"

"And did he say anything?"

"Naw, well, I don't remember now."

After soaking a bit of torn cotton about the size of a thumbnail in the cooled solution, he sank the tip of the needle into the center of the sodden wad. There was a faint noise, just like a baby sucking milk. The clear liquid filled the slender glass tube a little at a time. When he'd finished, Okinawa licked his lips and pressed the plunger very slightly to force the air out.

Reiko said, "Hey, let me do it, I'll shoot you up, Ryū. I used to do it for everybody back in Okinawa." Her sleeves were rolled up.

"Shit no! Not after what you did. You blew it that time and wasted a hundred dollars' worth. It's not like, you know, you're throwing together rice balls for a picnic or something. Fuck you. Here, tie Ryū's arm with this."

Reiko pouted and glared at Okinawa as she took the leather thong and made a tight tourniquet around my left arm. When I made a fist with my hand, a thick blood vessel stood out in my arm. Okinawa rubbed the spot with alcohol two or three times before plunging the wet needle tip in toward the bulging vein. When I opened my fist, blackish blood ran up into the cylinder. Saying Heyheyhey, Okinawa coolly pushed the plunger, and the heroin and blood entered me all at once.

"Hey, well, that's it, how about it?" Okinawa laughed. He pulled out the needle. In the instant that my skin quivered and the needle was gone, the smack had already rushed to my finger-tips and hit my heart with a dull thud. Before my eyes there seemed to be something like a white mist, and I couldn't make out Okinawa's face very well. I pressed my hand against my chest and stood up. I wanted to take a deep breath, but my breathing rhythm was off and I had trouble doing it. My head was numb as if it had been beaten, and the inside of my mouth was dry enough to burn. Reiko took my right shoulder to hold me up. When I tried to swallow just a little saliva from my dry gums, I was filled with a nausea that seemed to rush up from my feet. I fell groaning onto the bed.

Reiko seemed worried and shook my shoulder.

"Hey, don't you think you gave him a little too much? He hasn't shot up a lot before, hey look, he's real pale, is he O.K.?"

"I didn't give him that much, he's not gonna die, right? Naw, he's not gonna die, Reiko, but bring that pan, he's sure gonna heave."

I buried my face in the pillow. Although the back of my throat was parched, spittle overflowed steadily from my lips, and when I tried to lap some up with my tongue, violent nausea attacked my lower belly.

Even trying as hard as I could to breathe, I got only a little air, and that felt as if it didn't come in through my nose or mouth but just seeped in through a tiny hole in my chest. My hips were almost too numb to move. From time to time a strangling pain pierced my heart. The swollen veins in my temples twitched. When I closed my eyes, I felt panicky, as if I were being pulled at terrible speed into a lukewarm whirlpool. Clammy caresses ran all over my body, and I began to melt like cheese on a ham-burger. Like water and globs of oil in a test tube, distinct areas of hot and cold were shifting around in my body. In my head and throat and heart and prick, fevers were moving.

I tried to call Reiko, my throat cramped, no words came out.

I'd been thinking I wanted a cigarette, that's why I wanted to call Reiko, but when I opened my mouth my vocal cords just quivered and gave off a strange whistling sound. I could hear the clock ticking over near Okinawa and Reiko. The regular sound rang in my ear with a strange gentleness. I could scarcely see. At the right side of my range of vision, which was like a diffused reflection on water, there was a dazzling flicker that hurt me. As I thought that must be the candle, Reiko peered into my face and lifted my wrist to check my pulse, then said to Okinawa, He's not dead.

I moved my mouth desperately. Raising an arm as heavy as iron I touched Reiko's shoulder and whispered, "Give me a smoke." Reiko put a lighted cigarette between my lips, wet with spittle. She turned toward Okinawa and said, "Hey, look here at Ryū's eyes, he looks scared as a little kid, right? He's shaking, you know, it's really pathetic, hey, he's even crying."

The smoke clawing at my lungs was like a living thing. Okinawa took my chin in his hand to raise my face and check the pupils of my eyes and said to Reiko, "Hey, that was a close call, a real bummer, like, if he'd been maybe twenty pounds lighter that would've been the end of him." The warped outlines of his face looked like the sun seen through the beach umbrella you sprawl under in summer. I felt as if I'd become a plant. Folding its grayish leaves at dusk, never putting out flowers, just having its downy spores blown away by the wind, a quiet plant like a fern.

The light was put out. I could hear the sounds of Okinawa and Reiko undressing. The sound of the record rose—"Soft Parade" by The Doors—and between the notes I could hear rubbing on the rug and stifled moans from Reiko.

An image of a woman plunging from a tall building floated into my mind. She was staring at the receding sky, her face was distorted with terror. She made swimming motions, struggling to rise again. Her hair had come undone and waved above her head

17

like seaweed. The trees along the streets, the cars, the people growing larger, her nose and lips twisted by the wind pressure—the scene in my mind was just like the bad dreams that drench you with sweat in midsummer. It was a slow motion film in black and white—the movement of the woman, falling from the building.

They got up, wiped the sweat from each other, and lit the candle again. I turned away from the brightness. They were talking in voices too low for me to make out. From time to time I was seized with cramp and nausea. The nausea came in waves. Biting my lip, gripping the sheet, I rode it out, and when the nausea stopped at my head and rolled back again, I noticed a pleasure just like sexual release.

"Okinawa, you, you dirty rat!"

Reiko's high voice rang out. With it came the sound of breaking glass. One of them fell on the bed and the mattress sank down, tilting my body a little. The other one, it seemed to be Okinawa, spat out the word Shit!, yanked open the door and left. The candle was snuffed out in the wind and I could hear the sound of someone pounding down the iron staircase. In the pitch dark room I heard the soft sound of Reiko's breathing, and then I started to faint as I fought down the nausea. An odor just like the rotten pineapple, I could smell the same sweetish odor from the juices of this mixed-blood girl Reiko. I recalled the face of a certain woman. Long ago, I'd seen her in a movie or a dream, thin, long fingers and toes, slowly letting her slip fall from her shoulders, taking a shower behind a transparent wall, then, water dripping from her pointed chin, she gazed into her own green eyes in a mirror, a foreign woman.

The man walking ahead of us looked back and stopped, then tossed away a cigarette in the running water of the ditch. Firmly clutching a new duralumin crutch in his left hand, he moved on. Sweat ran down the back of his neck, and from the way he moved, I thought he must have hurt his leg just recently. His right arm seemed heavy and stiff, and there was a long groove in the earth where his foot had dragged.

The sun was straight overhead. Walking along, Reiko slipped off the jacket draped over her shoulders. Sweat blotched the tight blouse sticking to her body.

She seemed tired, as if she hadn't slept the night before. In front of a restaurant I said, ''Let's have something to eat.'' She just shook her head without answering.

''I don't understand that guy Okinawa—I mean, the trains had already stopped running for the night by the time he left.''

''It's O.K., Ryū, I've had enough,'' Reiko said softly. She pulled a leaf from a poplar tree planted beside the road.

''Hey, what do they call this thing like a line here, this here, do you know?''

The torn leaf was dusty.

''Isn't that a vein?''

''Yeah, that's it, a vein—me, I was taking biology in junior high, and I made a specimen book of these. I forget what it's called but I put on some kind of chemical, you know, and it just left these all white and dissolved the leaves, just left the veins real pretty.''

The man with the crutch sat down on the bench at the bus stop and looked at the schedule board. "Fussa General Hospital," the bus stop sign read. The big hospital building was on the left, and in its fan-shaped central garden, over ten patients in bathrobes were doing exercises, led by a nurse. They all had thick bandages on their ankles, and they twisted their hips and heads in time with the tweets of a whistle. People coming up to the hospital watched the patients.

"Hey, I'm coming over to your bar today, I want to tell Moko and Kei about the party. They'll be coming in today?"

"Sure they'll come, they come every day, so they'll come in today, too. . . . Me, I'd really like to show it to you."

"What?"

"That specimen book with all the leaves in it. A lot of people back in Okinawa collect insects, because they've got prettier butterflies than here, but me, I made a book of leaf veins, you know, and the teacher said it was real good, and because I got a prize and went all the way to Kagoshima, I still keep it in my desk drawer. I'm taking real good care of it, I really want to show it to you."

We reached the station, Reiko threw away the poplar leaf beside the road. The roof over the platform flashed silver, and I put on my sunglasses. "It's already summer, really hot."

"Huh? What?"

"Yeah, I said it's already summer."

"Summer's hotter." Reiko just stared at the rails.

Drinking wine at the counter, I could hear the sound of someone crunching a Nibrole pill in one corner of the bar.

After closing up early, Reiko had spilled about two hundred
Nibrole pills out onto the table. Kazuo said he'd lifted them from
a drugstore in Tachikawa. Then she said to everyone, Tonight's
the party before the party!

She got up on the counter, pulled off her stockings while dancing in time with the record music, came over to hug me and
stuck her tongue, smelling of the pills, into my mouth. Finally
she heaved up blackish blood and vomit and stretched out on the
sofa without moving. Yoshiyama, brushing back his long hair
with his hand, shaking droplets of water out of his beard, was
talking with Moko. She looked over at me, sticking her tongue
out and winking. Yoshiyama turned and asked me with a laugh,
Hey, Ryū, it's been awhile, you got anything for me? Any hash
or something? I put both elbows on the counter and let my feet,
in rubber sandals, dangle from the chair. My tongue smarted from
smoking too much. The sour wine stuck in my throat. Hey,
don't you have any sweeter wine?

Kei was telling Kazuo how she'd gone to Akita to work as a
nude model, but he looked drowsy from the Nibrole. Drinking
whiskey straight from the bottle, tossing peanuts one at a time
into her mouth, she said, So there Ah was, tied up on stage, it
was jes' awful, hey, Kazuo, tied up with some prickly rope—don'
ya think that was awful? Kazuo wasn't paying any attention to
her. He was peering at me through the finder of his Nikomat,

which he called "more precious than life itself." Hey, ya gotta listen when people are talking. With a poke in the back, Kei tumbled Kazuo onto the floor. Hey, wow, don't mess around, he said, that's a bummer, what if you'd broke it? Kei snickered, stripped off her blouse, started cheek-dancing and tongue-kissing with whoever she bumped into.

Maybe because of yesterday's heroin, I felt dragged out and didn't want any of the Nibrole. Moko came over. Hey, Ryū, won't you go in the can with me? Yoshiyama felt me up and I'm all shaky. She was wearing a red velvet dress and matching hat, and the powder smeared thickly around her eyes was red. Ryū, you remember when you made me in the can at that disco? Her eyes were bleary and unfocused. The tip of her tongue flicked from her lips and her voice was too sweet. Hey, you remember? You told me a big lie, said the cops had come and we had to hide, right? And got me all scrunched up in that little can—you've forgot?

Oh wow, that's the first time I've heard that one, Ryū, is that the way it was? You're a real stud, right? Even though you've got a face like a pot, you've done stuff like that, huh? Yeah, that's the first time I've heard. Yoshiyama's voice was loud. He let the needle fall on a record. What are you talking about, Moko, stop running off at the mouth, O.K.? It's just something she made up, Yoshiyama, I answered. With a blast of sound, Mick Jagger began to sing. It was a really old song, "Time Is on My Side." Moko threw one leg over my knees and said drunkenly, I hate lying, Ryū, don't lie, that time I came four times, four times, you know. I'm not going to forget or anything.

Reiko stood up, her face greenish pale, muttered, What time is it now, what time is it? to no one in particular, staggered to the counter, took the whiskey from Kei's hand, poured some down her throat, and had another violent fit of coughing. That's real dumb, Reiko, ya jes' lie down like a good girl. Kei grabbed back the whiskey roughly, wiped Reiko's spittle from the mouth of the bottle with her hand, and took another sip. When Kei pushed her on the chest, Reiko fell against the sofa, then turned to me and said, Hey, don't make it so loud, that's no good, the guys from the mahjongg place upstairs will get after me. They're real finks, they'll call the police, so can't you keep it down a little?

As I leaned over the amps to lower the sound, Moko squealed and jumped astride me. Her cold thighs squeezed my neck.

Hey, Moko, you wanna make it with Ryū that much? I'll do it for you, how about me?

I could hear Yoshiyama's voice behind me. I pinched Moko's thighs hard. She shrieked and tumbled to the floor. Idiot, freak, Ryū, you idiot, you can't even get it up, I'm sure you can't, I heard you're a fairy for those niggers, you've been taking too much dope! Maybe because it was too much trouble to rise, Moko lay where she had fallen, laughing, lashing out to kick my legs with her high heels.

Reiko pressed her face into the sofa and said in a low voice, Aww I wanna die, my chest hurts, hey my chest really hurts, me, I wanna die. Kei looked up from the Stones' record jacket she'd been reading and gazed at Reiko. Well, why don' ya jes' go ahead and die then? Hey, Ryū, that's right, huh? Ya think so? People who wanna die should jes' go ahead and die without a lot of fuss. It's real dumb, Reiko's jes' playing up to us.

Kazuo attached the strobe to his Nikomat and shot a picture of Kei. When the the strobe went off, Moko—lying flat on the floor—raised her head. Now Kazuo, cut that out, stop taking pictures without any say-so. Ah'm a pro and get a guaranteed wage. That real glittery light jes' gets me down, Ah hate photographs, so turn out that real glittery light, that's why ya don' get along with people.

Reiko groaned as if in pain, half-turned her body, and heaved up globs of vomit. Flustered, Kei ran to her, spread a newspaper, wiped her mouth with a towel, and massaged her back. There were a lot of rice grains in the vomit; I thought of the fried rice we'd eaten together that evening. The red ceiling light was reflected on the surface of the brownish vomit on the newspaper. Reiko, eyes closed, was mumbling, I wanna go home, me, I wanna go back there, I wanna go home. Yoshiyama pulled Moko to her feet and while he was undoing the buttons on the front of her dress, he chimed in on Reiko's monologue: Yeah, that's right, it's getting to be the best time of year to be in Okinawa, yeah. Moko grabbed Yoshiyama's hand as he tried to squeeze her breasts, then hugged Kazuo, saying, Hey, take a picture, in the same sugary voice. I'm in that fashion mag *An-An*, this month's issue, as a model, in color, hey Ryū, I guess you saw it?

Kei rubbed her finger, wet with Reiko's spittle, on her jeans and dropped the needle on a new record, "It's a Beautiful Day." Reiko's jes' playing up to us. Kazuo, his legs sprawled wide on the sofa, lay back and clicked the shutter at random. The strobe burned steadily, so I pressed my hands against my eyes. Hey, Kazuo, cut it out, you'll use up the battery.

Yoshiyama tried to kiss Kei but was pushed away. What is it with you? Didn't you say you were having the hots yesterday? When you fed the cat, you said Blackey, you and me really want it bad, huh? That's what you said, right? So how about a kiss?

Kei drank her whiskey.

Moko was posing in front of Kazuo, holding up her hair and grinning at him. Hey, you can't come up with a real smile now just by saying cheese, Moko.

Kei yelled at Yoshiyama. Ya're making such a fuss, jes' leave me alone, Ah get mad jes' seeing that face of yours. That pork cutlet ya ate for supper, ya know that money came from a farmer in Akita, the thousand yen he gave me with his hand all black, ya know that?

Moko looked at me and stuck out her tongue, I hate you, Ryū, you pervert.

Thirsty for some cold water, I chipped at the block of ice with an ice pick but stabbed my finger. Kei, who'd been dancing on the counter, ignoring Yoshiyama, got down and licked the blood welling out of that little hole, saying Ryū, so ya've given up music?

Reiko got up from the sofa and begged, Hey, please turn down the sound.

Nobody went near the amps.

The front of her dress gaping open, Moko came over to me as I pressed a paper napkin to my finger and asked, laughing, Ryū, how much can we get from those niggers?

Huh? You're talking about the party?

I mean if Kei or I make it with those niggers, how much can we get from them? I'm not saying it has anything to do with me, you know, but—

Sitting on the counter, Kei said, Ya jes' cut it out, Moko, that kind of killjoy talk, if ya want money Ah'll take ya to a good guy. A party's not for money, it's for having fun.

Moko twisted the gold chain dangling on my chest around her finger and sneered, I guess you got this from one of those niggers?

You dumb cunt, I got this in high school from a girl in my class, on her birthday. I played "A Certain Smile" for her and that got to her and she gave me this. She was a rich kid, her father had a big lumber yard. And listen, Moko, you've got to stop saying nigger, they'll kill you, they can understand that much Japanese. If you don't like it, you don't have to come along— right, Kei? There're plenty of other girls who want to come to our parties.

When she saw Kei nodding, her mouth full of whiskey, Moko said, Aww, don't get mad, I was just kidding. She hugged me.

I'll go, didn't we already decide that? Those niggers are strong and they'll give us some hash, right? She stuck her tongue in my mouth.

Kazuo brought the Nikomat up almost to my nose, and just as I yelled, Cut it out, he pressed the shutter. As if I'd been hit hard on the head, everything turned white before my eyes. I couldn't see. Moko clapped her hands and shrieked with laughter. I slid along the counter, almost falling, but Kei held me up and passed some whiskey from her mouth into mine. She'd smeared on sticky oily-smelly lipstick. The lipstick-flavored whiskey burned down my throat.

Bastard! Stop it, won't you cut it out? Yoshiyama yelled, slamming the comic book he'd been reading on the floor. Kei, you'd kiss Ryū, huh? I took a step and staggered, knocking over the table; there were the sounds of breaking glass, foaming beer, peanuts rolling on the floor. Reiko got up, shaking her head, and yelled, Everybody out! Get out! Rubbing my head I put some ice in my mouth and went over to her. Don't worry, Reiko, I'll clean up everything afterwards, it'll be O.K.

This is my place, tell everybody to get out! Hey Ryū, Ryū, it's O.K. if you stay, but tell the others to get out of here. Reiko squeezed my hand.

Yoshiyama and Kei were glaring at each other.

Hey, so you'll kiss Ryū instead of me? Huh?

Kazuo said timidly, Yoshiyama, I'm the one to blame, it's not like you think, I was fooling around with the strobe and got Ryū and he was falling over, so Kei gave him some whiskey, you know, like medicine. Yoshiyama growled, Get away, and shoved Kazuo, so that the Nikomat almost fell. Hey, what're you doing? Kazuo snapped. Caught in Kazuo's arms Moko mumbled, Wow, this is really dumb, right?

What's the matter, ya jealous? Kei made her dangling sandals slap against her feet. Eyes swollen from crying, Reiko pulled at my sleeve and said, Hey, get me some ice. I wrapped some up in a paper napkin and put it on her forehead. Kazuo turned to Yoshiyama, who had stood up and was glaring at Kei, and clicked the shutter again. Yoshiyama almost punched him. Moko laughed loudly.

Kazuo and Moko said they were going to clear out. We think we'll go to the bathhouse for a while, Moko said.

Hey, Moko, you'd better button up, or some punk'll paw you. And it's Kōenji Station tomorrow at one o'clock, so don't be late. Laughing, Moko answered, I know, you pervert, I won't forget or anything. I'm going to dress up really fine. Kazuo dropped to one knee on the road and clicked the shutter at me again.

A drunk who'd come along singing said something and turned back toward the strobe.

Reiko was trembling slightly. The paper napkin had fallen on the floor and the ice had almost all melted.

The way Ah'm feeling now doesn't have anything to do with you, Yoshiyama, it's jes' nothing much at all. Ah don't have to sleep with ya, right? Puffing her cigarette smoke straight up, Kei talked slowly to Yoshiyama. Anyway, ya jes' stop hassling me, jes' stop it. Ah don't care if we break up, ya might not like it but Ah'd be O.K. Anyway, ya want some more to drink? It's the party before the party, right, Ryū?

I sat down beside Reiko. When I put my hand on the back of her neck, her body jerked slightly and smelly saliva trailed from one side of her mouth.

Kei, you quit saying 'Ah' and stuff like that all the time. I don't like you to talk like that, so cut it out, huh? So O.K., I'll go start work tomorrow, that'll be O.K., right? I'll get together some bread, so it'll be O.K., huh?

Kei was sitting on the counter. Oh, is that so? Yeah, go to work, that'll really help me out. She swung her legs back and forth.

27

I don't give a damn if you try playing around, it's just your saying 'Ah' and stuff, it sort of gets to me. I'll just think it's because you have the hots, and anyway everything's gonna be fine because I'll go get a job on the docks in Yokohama, huh? Yoshiyama gripped Kei's leg. Her tight slacks were pasted on her thighs, the slight bulge of her belly rested on her belt.

What're ya talking about? Don't say crazy mixed-up stuff, it embarrasses me. Look, isn't Ryū laughing? Ah don't get what ya're saying at all, Ah'm jes' me, that's all.

Stop talking like that! Where'd you pick up that accent anyway?

Kei tossed her cigarette in the sink. Pulling on her shirt, she said, That's from mah own mama, didn't ya know Mama talks like this? Hey, didn't ya come to mah house one time, remember the woman with the cat, sitting in the *kotatsu*, munching on rice crackers? That's mah mama and she talks like Ah do, didn't ya hear her?

Yoshiyama bent down and asked me for a smoke, then dropped the Kool I tossed to him. Flustered he picked it up, slightly damp with beer, stuck it in his mouth, and, lighting it, said quietly, Let's go home.

Ya go home by y'self, Ah'm O.K. here.

Wiping Reiko's mouth, I asked Yoshiyama, Aren't you coming to the party tomorrow?

Ah think it's O.K. if he doesn't, isn't it O.K.? This guy says he's going to work so it's O.K. if he works. It won't matter any if Yoshiyama's there or not, will it? Ya just go back to our place, if ya don't go back soon, ya won't be able to get up. Tomorrow's Yokohama, right? Early?

Hey Yoshiyama, you really don't plan to come?

Without answering he went over to one corner of the room and started to put "Left Alone" on the spinning turntable.

As he pulled the record from its jacket, which had a ghostly photo of Billy Holiday, Kei got down off the counter and said in his ear, Make it the Stones.

Cut it out, Kei, don't talk to me anymore.

Yoshiyama looked straight at her, cigarette clamped tight in his mouth.

It's so dumb, what's with that record, ya want to listen to gloomy piano again, right, just like a tired old granddaddy? That stuff is to blacks like what *Naniwabushi* is to us. Hey, Ryū, say something to him, this is the latest Rolling Stones, ya haven't heard it, have ya? It's 'Sticky Fingers.'

Ignoring her, Yoshiyama put Mal Waldron on the turntable.

Kei, it's already late and Reiko told us to keep it down. And it's no good playing the Stones with the sound turned down, right?

Buttoning her shirt and looking in the mirror to fix her hair, Kei asked, What about tomorrow?

We decided on one o'clock at Kōenji Station, I answered. Kei nodded, smeared on some lipstick.

Yoshiyama, Ah'm not coming back tonight because Ah'm going to Sam's place, so be sure and give the cat some milk, not the milk in the refrigerator, the milk on the shelf, don't mix them up.

Yoshiyama didn't answer.

When Kei opened the door, the air that flowed in was cool and moist. Hey, Kei, leave it open for a while.

As we listened to ''Left Alone'' Yoshiyama filled a tumbler with gin. I picked up the pieces of glass scattered on the floor and collected them on the newspaper soaked with Reiko's vomit. ''I don't like to say it, but these days it always goes like that,'' Yoshiyama muttered as he stared at the ceiling.

''It was the same even before she went up to Akita to work, we sleep separate at night, even though I don't do it much anyway.''

I drank a coke from the refrigerator. Yoshiyama waved his hand to show he didn't want any and drained down all the gin.

"She's been saying she wants to go to Hawaii. It's been awhile but remember about how there was talk maybe her dad is in Hawaii? I thought I'd get together some bread and send her there, well, I don't know if the guy in Hawaii is really her dad or not, but . . .

"I thought I'd work, get together some bread, but now everything's all mixed up and I don't have a clue what she's thinking anymore, she's like that all the time, every day."

Yoshiyama pressed his hand to his chest, stood up, and hurried outside, I could hear him spewing into the gutter. Reiko was really passed out. She was breathing through her mouth. From the back cupboard, hidden behind a curtain, I took a blanket and covered her with it.

He came back holding his belly, wiping his mouth with his shirt cuff. Yellow vomit clung to the front of his rubber sandals, a sour smell floated from his body. I could hear Reiko's faint breathing.

"Yoshiyama, come tomorrow, to the party."

"Yeah, well, Kei, she's looking forward to it, says she wants to do it with those niggers again, so I'm kind of . . . you know.

"What's with Reiko today? She was pretty wild." Yoshiyama sat down opposite me and swallowed a mouthful of gin.

"Yesterday, at my place, she had a fight with Okinawa. She didn't get to shoot up, you know. She's fat and her veins don't stand out, I guess, and Okinawa got impatient and shot it all up himself, hers too, shot it all up."

"Real idiots, they are. And you were watching like an idiot?"

"No, I'd shot up. I was flat out on the bed, thought maybe I'd die. It was scary, I got a little too much, really scary."

Yoshiyama took two more Nibrole pills, dissolved in gin.

My stomach felt empty but I didn't feel like eating. Thinking maybe at least I'd have some soup I looked in the pan on the gas ring, but the surface of the soup was a film of gray mold, and the bean curd in it was slimy, rotten.

Since Yoshiyama said he'd really like some coffee, with a lot of milk, I put up with the awful smell of the soup and warmed some coffee in a pot.

Yoshiyama poured milk up to the brim of his cup, held it firmly in both hands, and brought it to his mouth. He yelled, Hot! and vomit sprayed from his pursed lips like water from a toy pistol and fell in globs on the counter.

"Aw shit, I'll just stick with liquor," he said, and gulped down the gin left in his glass. When he had a slight fit of coughing and I rubbed his back, he turned around and said, You're really great. His lips twisted. His back, sticky and cold, had a sour smell.

"After that I went back to Toyama, I guess you heard from Reiko? After I'd been at your place, my mom died, I guess you heard?"

I nodded. Yoshiyama's glass was full of gin again. The too-sweet coffee stabbed my roughened tongue.

"It's really a funny feeling when somebody actually dies on you, that was the first time for me. Are your folks O.K., Ryū?"

"They're O.K., they worry about me, I get all kinds of letters."

The last number on "Left Alone" ended. The record turned with the sound of tearing cloth.

"Yeah, well anyway, I took Kei with me, she said she'd come along to Toyama, she didn't want to stay at our place by herself. Sure, don't you get how she felt? We stayed at this inn but it was ¥2000 without meals, really high."

I turned off the stereo. Reiko's feet stuck out from under the blanket, the soles were black with dirt.

"And then on the day of the funeral, you know, Kei phoned

me, said to come back over for a while because she was lonely. When I said how can I leave, she said she'd just kill herself and so I was really freaked and I went. She was listening to an old radio in that dirty six-mat room. She said she couldn't get the FEN station, well, how can you expect to get the GI broadcasts way over in Toyama? And then she asked me all sorts of stuff about my mom, really dumb stuff. She was laughing in this fakey way, it was a bad scene, honestly. When she'd died—Kei asked how my mom's face had looked when she'd died, and is it really true they put makeup on people before putting them in coffins, stuff like that, you know. When I said, Yeah, they put makeup on her, she asked, What brand? Max Factor? Revlon? Kanebo? How was I supposed to know something like that? And then she started sniffling, said she'd been really lonely, then she bawled, you know."

"But, well, I think I understand how she felt, waiting around on that kind of a day, yeah, I know it'd be lonely."

The sugar had sunk to the bottom of the coffee; I swallowed without thinking. All at once the inside of my mouth was coated with sugar and I felt sick.

"Yeah, I see that, too. I know, but listen, my own mom was really dead. Kei was crying and mumbling and then she dragged the bedding out of the closet and she stripped. I mean, I'd just said good-bye to my dead mother and there I was being grabbed by this naked half-blood chick. It was kind of, Ryū, you know what I mean? It would have been O.K., I guess, if we'd done it, but it was kind of, you know, kind of . . . "

"You didn't, huh?"

"How could I? Kei was bawling, and I actually got uptight, hey, you know the soap operas on TV? Somehow I felt I was in one of those soap operas, I got worried maybe they could hear us in the next room, I was ashamed. I wonder what Kei was thinking then—anyway, it's been no good between us ever since."

The only sound was Reiko's breathing. The dusty blanket moved up and down in time with it. Sometimes drunks peered in through the open door.

"Anyway, ever since, it's been weird. Yeah, we fought a lot before.

"But now somehow, you know, it's different. Somehow, something's different.

"And even though we'd talked about Hawaii before and been making plans for a long time, you saw how it was today?

"Yeah, even sex is no good anymore, I'd be better off going to one of those Turkish baths."

"Your mother, was she sick?"

"I guess you could say that, her body was just worn out. Her eyes were all tired, like, and she'd gotten a lot smaller than she used to be. When she died. Yeah, it was pretty sad about my mom, I felt it didn't have anything much to do with me, but it was pretty sad.

"Did you know? She went around peddling that old-time Toyama medicine. When I was little I went around a lot with her. She'd walk around all day with that bundle as big as an icebox on her back. There're regular customers for it all over the country, you know? And do you know those paper balloons, the kind you can blow into and puff up, she used to give them out free. I used to play around a lot with those.

"It's really funny, when I think about it now. It was really something—I could play all day with a thing like that. If I tried it now, I'd be bored stiff, but even back then I was bored, really, I don't remember having any fun. One time I was waiting for my mom in this inn, you know, and the electric light was out, and I realized the sun had set and it was getting dark. I couldn't say anything to the maids there, I wasn't even in grade school, I was scared. I went over to one corner of the room where a little light came in from the street—I can't forget it, I really was scared, that little street, and the town smelling of fish. I wonder where it was, the whole town smelled of fish, where was it?"

There was the sound of a car far off. Reiko mumbled now and then. Yoshiyama went outside again. I followed. Side by side, we puked into the gutter. I braced my left hand against a wall and stuck my finger back into my throat; the muscles of my stomach jerked and warm fluid came out. As waves passed though my chest and belly, sour lumps lodged in my throat and mouth, and when I pushed them with my tongue, they numbed my gums and then plopped into the water.

As we walked back inside, Yoshiyama said, "Hey, Ryū, when I heave like that, you know, and my guts are all mixed up and I can hardly stay on my feet and I can't see good, you know, that's the only time I really want a woman. Well, even if there was one around, I couldn't get it up and it'd be too much trouble to open her legs, but anyway I still want a woman. Not in my prick or in my head, but my whole body, all of me, is just squirming for it. How about you? Do you get what I mean?"

"Yeah, you want to kill her, rather then fuck her?"

"That's it, that's it, squeezing her neck like this, tearing her clothes off, ramming a stick or something up her butt, a classy chick like the kind you see walking on the Ginza."

Reiko was coming out of the john; she said sleepily Hi, come in. The front of her slacks was open.

She seemed about to fall; I ran forward and held her up.

"Thanks, Ryū, it's quiet now, isn't it? Hey, give me some water. My mouth's sticky—" Her head dropped. As I cracked some ice, Yoshiyama was stripping her where she lay on the sofa.

The Nikomat lens reflected a dark sky and small sun. When I bent forward to have it reflect my face, Kei bumped into me.

"Ryū, what're ya doing?"

"Who's talking, you're the last one here, it's no good being late."

"On the bus, ya know, this old guy spat on the floor and the driver made a fuss about it, even stopped the bus. They both got red in the face, shouting at each other, even though it's so hot. Where's everybody?"

Yoshiyama was sitting sleepily by the street. She laughed at him. "Hey, weren't ya going to Yokohama today?"

Reiko and Moko finally came out of the clothes shop in front of the station. Everybody around turned to look at Reiko. She was wearing an Indian dress she'd just bought, a red silk dress covered with tiny round mirrors all the way down to the ankles.

"You really got another wild outfit," Kazuo laughed, turned his Nikomat on her.

Kei said in my ear—her perfume hit me—"Hey, Ryū, Ah wonder if she doesn't know, being that fat and buying that kind of dress."

"It doesn't matter, does it? She must have wanted to change her mood. She'll get tired of it soon, you can get it from her then, Kei, it'd be sure to look good on you."

Glancing around, Reiko said to us all in a tiny voice, "Me, I was shocked. Moko did it right while the store clerks are watching, stuffed it in her bag all at once."

"What, Moko, you've been lifting stuff again? You're stoned? They'll get you if you don't cut it out," Yoshiyama said, screwing up his face against the fumes from a bus. Moko thrust her arm in front of my face.

"Smell's good, huh? Dior."

"Dior's O.K., but don't be such a show-off about your lifting, you'll get us all in trouble."

While Yoshiyama and Kazuo went off to buy hamburgers, the three girls exchanged cosmetics and smeared their faces, leaning against the railing by the ticket puncher. They pouted and peered into their compact mirrors. People passing by looked at them strangely.

An older station official laughed to Reiko, "Great clothes, sister, where're you going?"

Drawing on her eyebrows and looking very serious, she told the man who punched her ticket, "Party, we're going to a party now."

In the middle of Oscar's room, nearly a fistful of hashish smoldered in an incense burner, and like it or not, the spreading smoke
entered one's chest with every breath. In less than thirty seconds
I was completely stoned. I felt as if my insides were oozing out
through every pore, and other people's sweat and breath were
flowing in.

Especially the lower half of my body felt heavy and sore, as if
sunk into thick mud, and my mouth itched to hold somebody's
prick and drain it. While we ate the fruit piled on plates and
drank wine, the whole room was raped by heat. I wanted my
skin peeled off. I wanted to take in the greased, shiny bodies
of the black men and rock them inside of me. Cherry cheesecake, grapes in black hands, steaming boiled crab legs breaking
with a snap, clear sweet pale purple American wine, pickles like
dead men's wart-covered fingers, bacon sandwiches like the
mouths of women, salad dripping pink mayonnaise.

Bob's huge cock was stuffed all the way into Kei's mouth.

Ah'm jes' gonna see who's got the biggest. She crawled around
on the rug like a dog and did the same for everyone.

Discovering that the largest belonged to a half-Japanese named
Saburō, she took a cosmos flower from an empty vermouth bottle
and stuck it in as a trophy.

Hey, Ryū, his is twice the size of the one ya got.

Saburō raised his head and let out an Indian yell, then Kei
seized the cosmos flower between her teeth and pulled it out,
jumped on the table, and shook her hips, like a Spanish dancer.

Flashing blue strobe lights circled the ceiling. The music was a luxuriant samba by Luiz Bon Fa. Kei shook her body violently, hot after seeing the wetness on the flower.

Somebody do it to me, do it to me quick, Kei yelled in English, and I don't know how many black arms reached out to throw her on the sofa and tear off her slip, the little pieces of black translucent cloth fluttering to the floor. Hey, just like butterflies, said Reiko, taking a piece of the cloth and spreading butter on Durham's prick. After Bob yelled and thrust his hand into Kei's crotch, the room filled with shrieks and shrill laughter.

Looking around the room, watching the twisting bodies of the three Japanese girls, I drank peppermint wine and munched crackers spread with honey.

The penises of the black men were so long they looked slender. Even fully erect, Durham's bent fairly far as Reiko twisted it. His legs trembled and he shot off suddenly, and everyone laughed at the sight of his come wetting the middle of Reiko's face. Reiko laughed too and blinked, but as she looked around for some tissue paper to wipe her face, Saburō easily picked her up. He pulled her legs open, just as if he were helping a little girl to piss, and lifted her onto his belly. His huge left hand gripping her head and his right pinning her ankles together, he held her so that all her weight hung on his cock. Reiko yelled, That hurts, and struck out with her hands, trying to pull away, but she couldn't grab on to anything.

Her face was getting pale.

Saburō, moving and spreading his legs to get more friction on his cock, leaned back against the sofa until he was lying almost flat and began to rotate Reiko's body, using her butt as a pivot.

On the first turn her entire body convulsed and she panicked. Her eyes bulging and her hands over her ears, she began to shriek like the heroine of a horror movie.

Saburō's laugh was like an African way cry, as Reiko twisted her face and clawed at her chest. Squeal some more, he said in Japanese, and began to turn her body faster. Oscar, who'd been sucking Moko's tits, Durham, who'd placed a cold towel on his wilted prick, Jackson, who wasn't naked yet, Bob on top of Kei— all gazed at the revolving Reiko. God! Outasight! said Bob and Durham, and went over to help turn her around. Bob took her feet and Durham her head; both pressing hard on her butt, they began to spin her faster. Laughing, showing his white teeth, Saburō then put both hands behind his head and arched his body to drive his cock in even deeper. Reiko suddenly burst into loud sobs. She bit her own fingers and tore at her hair, because of the spinning her tears flew outward without reaching her cheeks. We laughed harder than ever. Kei waved a piece of bacon and drank wine, Moko buried her red fingernails in the huge butt of wiry-haired Oscar. Reiko's toes were stretched back and quivering. Her cunt, rubbed hard, gaped red and shone with mucus. Saburō took deep breaths and slowed down the spinning, moving her in time with Luiz Bon Fa's singing of "Black Orpheus." I turned down the volume and sang along. Laughing all the time, Kei licked my toes while lying on her stomach on the rug. Reiko kept on crying, Durham's semen dried on her face. With bloody tooth marks on his fingers, sometimes growling like a lion from the pit of his stomach—Oh-h, I'm gonna bust, get this cunt off me, Saburō said in Japanese and thrust Reiko aside. Get away from me, pig! he yelled. Reiko grabbed at his legs as she fell forward; his come shot straight up and splattered and stayed on her back and buttocks. Reiko's belly quivered and some urine leaked out. Kei—she'd been smearing her own tits with honey— hurriedly slid some newspaper under Reiko.

That's jes' awful, she said, slapped Reiko's butt and laughed shrilly. Moving about the room, twisting our bodies, we took into ourselves the tongues and fingers and pricks of whoever we wanted.

I wonder where I am, I kept thinking. I put some of the grapes scattered on the table in my mouth. As I skinned them with my tongue and spat the seeds into a plate, my hand felt a cunt; when I looked up, Kei was standing there with her legs apart, grinning at me. Jackson stood up dazedly and stripped off his uniform. Grinding out the slim menthol cigarette he'd been smoking, he turned toward Moko, who was rocking away on top of Oscar. Dribbling a sweet-smelling fluid from a little brown bottle on Moko's butt, Jackson called, Hey, Ryū, bring me that white tube in my shirt pocket, O.K.? Her hands held tightly by Oscar, her bottom smeared with the cream, Moko let out a shriek: That's co-old! Jackson grasped and raised her buttocks, got his cock—also thickly coated with the cream—into position and began thrusting. Moko hunched over and screeched.

Kei looked up and came over, saying, That looks kind of fun.

Moko was crying. Kei grabbed her hair and peered into her face. Ah'll put some nice mentholatum on ya afterwards, Moko. Kei tongue-kissed with Oscar and laughed loudly again. With a pocket camera, I took a close-up of Moko's distorted face. Her nose was twitching like a long-distance runner making a last spurt. Reiko finally opened her eyes. Perhaps realizing that she was all sticky, she started for the shower. Her mouth was open, her eyes vacant, she tripped again and again and fell. When I put my hands on her shoulders to lift her up, she brought her face close to mine. Oh, Ryū, save me, she said. An odd smell came from her body. I dashed to the toilet and threw up. As Reiko sat on the tiles getting drenched by the shower, I couldn't tell which way her reddened eyes were looking.

Reiko, ya big dummy, ya'll jes' drown. Kei shut off the shower, thrust her hand in Reiko's crotch, then squealed with laughter to see Reiko jump up in panic. Oh, it's Kei. Reiko hugged her and kissed her on the lips. Kei beckoned to me as I sat on the toilet. Hey Ryū, that cold feels good, right? Since I was cold outside, I felt hotter inside. Hey, ya got a cute one. She took it in her mouth as Reiko pulled back my wet hair, sought out my tongue like a baby seeking the breast, and sucked hard. Kei braced her hands against the wall and thrust out her butt, then buried me in her hole, washed free of mucus by the shower and dried. Bob, his hands dripping sweat, came into the shower. There're not enough chicks, Ryū, you bastard, taking two of them.

Swatting my cheek, he roughly dragged us, dripping, just as we were, into the next room and threw us on the floor. My prick, still tight inside Kei, twisted as we fell. I groaned. Reiko was tossed like a rugby pass up on the bed and Bob leaped on top of her. She struggled, raving, but she was pinned down by Saburō and a chunk of cheesecake was crammed into her mouth, choking her. The record music changed to Osibisa. Moko wiped her butt, her face twitching. There were traces of blood on the paper. She showed them to Jackson and muttered, That's awful. Hey Reiko, that cheesecake's good, huh? Kei asked, lying on her stomach on the table. Reiko answered, Something's thrashing around in my stomach, like I'd swallowed a live fish or something. I got up on the bed to take her picture, but Bob bared his teeth and pushed me off. Rolling to the floor I bumped into Moko. Ryū, I hate that guy, I've had it, he's a fag, right? Moko was on top of Oscar, who rocked her while he gnawed a piece of chicken. She started to cry again.

Moko, you're O.K.? It doesn't hurt? I asked. Oh, I don't know anymore, Ryū, I just don't know.

She was rocked in time with the Osibisa record. Kei sat on Jackson's knee, sipping wine, talking about something. After rubbing her body with a piece of bacon, Jackson sprinkled on vanilla extract. A hoarse voice yelled Oh baby. A lot of stuff had ended up on the red rug. Underwear and cigarette ashes, scraps of bread and lettuce and tomato, different kinds of hair, blood-smeared paper, tumblers and bottles, grape skins, matches, dusty cherries—Moko staggered to her feet. Her hand on her ass, she said, I'm famished, and walked to the table. Jackson leaned over to apply a band-aid and a kiss.

Pressing her chin on the table, breathing hard, Moko attacked a crab like a starving child. Then one of the blacks stuck his shaft in front of her, and she took that in her mouth too. Stroking it with her tongue, she pushed it aside and turned again to the crab. The red shell crunched between her teeth, she pulled out the white meat with her hands. Piling it with pink mayonnaise from a plate, she put it on her tongue, the mayonnaise dribbling onto her chest. The odor of crab flowed through the room. On the bed, Reiko was still howling. Durham pushed up into Moko from behind. Her butt jiggled, she held onto the crab, her face twisted, she tried to drink some wine but with the rocking of her body it went into her nose and she choked, tears in her eyes. Seeing that, Kei laughed loudly. James Brown began to sing. Reiko crawled to the table, drained a glass of peppermint wine and said loudly, That tastes good.

"Haven't I told you over and over not to get in too deep with that Jackson, the MP's are watching him, he's going to get caught one of these days," Lilly said as she snapped off the TV picture of a young man singing.

Oscar had said, O.K., let's finish up, and opened the veranda doors. A piercing cold wind blew in, a fresh wind, which I could still feel.

But while everyone was still lying around naked, Bob's woman Tami had come in and gotten into a bad fight with Kei, who'd tried to stop her from hitting Bob. Tami's brother was a big gangster, and since she'd wanted to run and tell him, there was nothing I could do but bring her along here to Lilly's place. I'd heard Lilly was a friend of hers, she'd talk her around. Until just a few minutes ago, Tami had been sitting over there on the sofa, howling, I'll kill them! Her side had been raked by Kei's nails.

"So don't I always say you better not bring in punks who don't know anything about this Yokota territory? What would you have done without me, huh? You wouldn't have got off easy, Ryū, Tami's brother is real bad."

She drank a swallow from a glass of Coca-cola with a lemon slice floating in it, then passed it over to me. She brushed her hair and changed into a black negligee. Still seeming angry, she brushed her teeth and shot up on Philopon in the kitchen with the toothbrush still in her mouth.

"Aw, come off it, Lilly, I'm sorry."

"Oh, all right, I know you'll just go and do the same thing tomorrow. . . . But listen, you know, the waiter at my place, a guy from Yokosuka, is asking if I want to buy some mesc. How about it, Ryū? You want to try it, don't you?"

"How much is it, for one tab?"

"I don't know, he just said five dollars, should I buy it?"

Even Lilly's pubic hair was dyed to match. They don't sell stuff to dye the hair down here in Japan, she'd told me, I had to send away for it myself, got it from Denmark.

Through the hair over my eyes, I could see the ceiling light.

"Hey, Ryū, I had a dream about you," Lilly said, placing her hand around my neck.

"The one about me riding a horse in a park? I've heard that one before." I ran my tongue along Lilly's eyebrows, which were growing out again.

"No, another one, after the one in the park. The two of us go to the ocean, you know, a real pretty seaside. There's this big beach, wide and sandy, nobody there except you and me. We swim and play in the sand but then on the other side of the water we can see this town. Well, it's far away, so we shouldn't be able to see much, but we can even make out the faces of the people living there—that's how dreams are, right? First they're having some kind of celebration, some kind of foreign festival. But then, after a while, a war starts in that town, with artillery going boom, boom. A real war—even though it's so far away, we can see the soldiers and the tanks.

"So the two of us, you and me, Ryū, just watch from the beach, sort of dreamy like. And you say, Hey, wow, so that's war, and I say Yeah, right."

"You sure have some weird dreams, Lilly."

The bed was damp. Some feathers sticking out of the pillow pricked the back of my neck. I pulled out a little one and stroked Lilly's thighs with it.

The room was dimly gray. Some light stole in from the kitchen. Lilly was still asleep, her little hand, with the nail polish off, resting on my chest. Her cool breath brushed my armpit. The oval mirror hanging from the ceiling reflected our nakedness.

The night before, after we'd done it, Lilly had shot up again, humming deep in her white throat.

I just keep using more, no matter what, I've got to cut down pretty soon or I'll be an addict, right? she'd said, checking the amount left.

While Lilly had been rocking her body on top of mine, I'd remembered the dream she'd told me about, and also the face of a certain woman. As I'd watched the twisting of Lilly's slim hips . . .

The face of a thin woman digging a hole right next to a barbed wire entanglement around a large farm. The sun was sinking. The face of a woman bent down to thrust a shovel into the earth, beside a tub full of grapes, as a young soldier threatened her with his bayonet. The face of a woman wiping away her sweat with the back of her hand, hair hanging over her face. As I'd watched Lilly panting, the woman's face floated through my mind.

Damp air from the kitchen.

Is it raining? I wondered. The scene outside the window was smoky, milk colored. I noticed the front door was ajar. Yesterday, since we were both drunk, we must have gone to bed without closing it. A single high-heeled shoe lay on its side on the kitchen floor. The tapering heel stuck out, and the curve of firm leather over the front was as smooth as part of a woman.

Outside, in the narrow space I could see through the open door, stood Lilly's yellow Volkswagen. Raindrops stuck to it like goose bumps, and then the heavier ones slid down slowly, insects in winter.

People passing like shadows. A mailman in a blue uniform pushing a bicycle, several school children with book bags, a tall American with a Great Dane—all passing through the narrow space.

Lilly took a deep breath and half turned her body. She gave a low moan and the light blanket that had covered her fell to the floor. Her long hair stuck to her back in an S shape. The small of her back was sweaty.

Scattered on the floor was Lilly's underwear from the day before. Far away and rolled up small, the garments were just like little burn marks or dyed spots on the rug.

A Japanese woman with a black shoulder bag looked around the room from the doorway. Her cap bore some company insignia, the shoulders of her navy jacket were damp—I thought she must have come to read the gas or electric meter. When her eyes got used to the dim light, she noticed me, started to speak, seemed to think better of it, and stepped outside again. She glanced back once more at me, naked and smoking a cigarette, then went off toward the right, her head cocked to one side.

Through the space outside the door, now open a little wider, passed two grade-school girls, talking, gesturing, wearing red rubber boots. A black soldier in uniform ran by, leaping over the muddy spots just like a basketball player dodging a guard to shoot.

Beyond Lilly's car, on the other side of the street, stood a small black building. Its paint was peeling in places; ''U–37'' was written in orange.

Against the background of that black wall, I could clearly see the fine rain falling. Over the roof were heavy clouds, looking as if someone had smeared on layer after layer of gray pigment. The sky in the narrow rectangle that was visible to me was the brightest part.

Thick clouds swollen with fever. They made the air damp, made Lilly and me sweat. That's why the crumpled sheets were clammy.

A thin black line slanted across the narrow sky.

Maybe that's an electric wire, I thought, or a tree branch, but then it rained harder and soon I couldn't see it anymore.

The people walking in the street hurriedly put up umbrellas and began to run.

Puddles appeared on the muddy street even as I watched and widened out in a series of ripples. Played on by the rain, a big white car moved slowly along the street, almost filling it. Inside were two foreign women, one adjusting her hairnet in the mirror, and the other, the driver, watching the road so carefully that her nose was almost pressed against the windshield. Both were heavily made up; their dry skin appeared to be caked with powder.

A girl licking an ice cream bar passed, then came back and peered in. Her soft, blonde hair was plastered to her head, and she took Lilly's bath towel off the kitchen chair and began to wipe herself dry. She licked ice cream off her finger and sneezed. When she raised her head, she noticed me. Picking up the blanket and covering myself, I waved at her. She smiled and pointed outside. Putting my finger to my lips, I signaled her to keep quiet. Looking toward Lilly, I laid my head on my hand to show she was still sleeping. So be quiet, I gestured again, my finger to my lips, and grinned at her. The girl turned toward the outside and gestured with the hand holding the ice cream. I turned my palm upward and looked up in a pantomime of noticing the rain. The girl nodded, shaking her wet hair. Then she dashed outside and came back drenched, carrying a dripping bra that looked like one of Lilly's.

47

"Lilly, hey, it's raining, do you have washing hanging out? Get up, Lilly, it's raining!"

Rubbing her eyes, Lilly got up, saw the girl, hid herself behind the blanket, and said, "Hey, Sherry, what are you up to?" The girl tossed the bra she was holding, yelled in English "Rainy!" and laughed as her eyes met mine.

Even when I gently peeled the band-aid off her ass, Moko didn't open her eyes.

Reiko was rolled up in a blanket on the kitchen floor, Kei and Yoshiyama were on the bed, Kazuo was by the stereo, still holding tight to his Nikomat, Moko lay on her stomach on the carpet, hugging a pillow. There was a slight bloodstain on the band-aid I'd peeled off, the hurt place opened and closed as she breathed, reminding me of a rubber tube.

The sweat beading her back smelled just like sex juices.

When Moko opened the eye that still had false eyelashes, she grinned at me. Then she moaned when I put my hand between her buttocks and half turned her body.

You're lucky it's raining, rain's good for healing, I'll bet it doesn't hurt much because of the rain.

Moko's sticky crotch. I wiped it for her with soft paper, and when I stuck in a finger, her naked buttocks jiggled.

Kei opened her eyes and asked, Hey, so ya stayed over last night with that whore-lady?

Shut up, stupid, she's not like that, I said, swatting at the little insects flying around.

Ah mean Ah don' care, Ryū, but ya got to watch about getting a dose, like Jackson said, some of the guys around here have got it real bad, ya could rot to pieces. Kei pulled on just her panties and fixed coffee, Moko stretched out a hand and said, Hey, give me a smoke, one of those mint-flavor Sah-lem.

Moko, that's Say-lem, not Sah-lem, Kazuo told her, getting up.

Rubbing his eyes, Yoshiyama said loudly to Kei, No milk in mine, O.K.? Then he turned to me—my finger still in Moko's ass—and said, Last night when you guys were messing around upstairs, I got a straight flush, you know, really right on, a straight flush in hearts—Hey, Kazuo, you were there, you can back me up, right?

Without answering him, Kazuo said sleepily, My strobe's gone somewhere, somebody hiding it?

Jackson said I should wear makeup again, like I'd done before. That time, I thought maybe Faye Dunaway'd come to visit, Ryū, he said.

I put on a silver negligee Saburō said he'd got from a pro stripper.

Before everybody arrived in Oscar's room, a black man I'd never seen before came and left nearly a hundred capsules; I couldn't tell what they were. I asked Jackson if he might have been an M.P. or a C.I.D. man, but Jackson laughed, shaking his head, and answered, Naw, that's Green Eyes.

"You saw how his eyes are green? Nobody knows his real name, I heard he'd been a high school teacher but I don't know if it's true or not. He's crazy, really, we don't know where he lives or whether he has a family, just that he's been here a lot longer than we have, seems he's been in Japan an awful long time. Don't he look like Charlie Mingus? Maybe he came after he'd heard something about you. He say anything to you?"

That black man had looked very uptight. I'll give you just this much, he'd said, then rolled his eyes around the room and left as if he were making an escape.

His face hadn't changed even when he saw Moko was naked, and when Kei asked him, How about some fun? his lips had trembled but he didn't say anything.

"You'll get to see the black bird sometime, too, you haven't seen it yet, but you, you'll be able to see the bird, you've got them kind of eyes, same as me." Then he'd gripped my hand.

Oscar said not to take any of those capsules, because Green Eyes had once passed around laxatives. He told me to throw them out.

Jackson sterilized a battlefield syringe. I'm a medic, he said, so I'm a real pro at shots, right?

First they shot me up with heroin.

"Ryū, dance!" Jackson slapped my butt. When I stood up and looked in the mirror, I saw what looked like a different person, transformed by Moko's painstaking, expert makeup technique. Saburō passed me a cigarette and an artificial rose and asked, What music? I said make it Schubert and everyone laughed.

A sweet-smelling mist floated before my eyes and my head was heavy and numb. As I slowly moved my arms and legs, I felt that my joints had been oiled, and that slippery oil flowed around inside my body. As I breathed I forgot who I was. I thought that many things gradually flowed from my body, I became a doll. The room was full of sweetish air, smoke clawed my lungs. The feeling that I was a doll became stronger and stronger. All I had to do was just move as they wanted, I was the happiest possible slave. Bob muttered Sexy, Jackson said Shut up. Oscar put out all the lights and turned an orange spot on me. Once in a while my face twisted and I felt panicky. I opened my eyes wide and shook my body. I called out, panted low, licked jam off my finger, sipped wine, pulled up my hair, grinned, rolled up my eyes, spit out the words of a spell.

I yelled some lines I remembered by Jim Morrison: "When the music is over, when the music is over, put out all the lights, my brothers live at the bottom of the sea, my sister was killed, pulled up on land like a fish, her belly torn open, my sister was killed, when the music is over, put out all the lights, put out all the lights."

Like the splendid men in Genet's novels, I rolled saliva around in my mouth and put it on my tongue—dirty white candy. I rubbed my legs and clawed my chest my hips and my toes were sticky. Gooseflesh wrapped my body like a sudden wind and all my strength was gone.

I stroked the cheek of a black woman sitting with her knees drawn up next to Oscar. She was sweating, the toenails at the end of her long legs were painted silver.

A flabby fat white woman Saburō had brought along gazed at me, her eyes moist with desire. Jackson shot heroin into the palm of Reiko's hand; maybe it hurt, her face twitched. The black woman was already drunk on something. She put her hands under my armpits and made me stand up, then stood up herself and began to dance. Durham put hash in the incense burner again. The purple smoke rose and Kei crouched down to suck it in. At the smell of the black woman, clinging to me with her sweat, I almost fell. The smell was fierce, as if she were fermenting inside. She was taller than I, her hips jutted out, her arms and legs were very slender. Her teeth looked disturbingly white as she laughed and stripped. Lighter colored, pointed breasts didn't bounce much even when she shook her body. She seized my face between her hands and thrust her tongue into my mouth. She rubbed my hips, undid the hooks of the negligee, and ran her sweaty hands over my belly. Her rough tongue licked around my gums. Her smell completely enveloped me; I felt nauseated.

Kei came crawling over and gripped my cock, saying, Do it right, Ryū, get it up. All at once spittle gushed from one corner of my mouth down to my chin and I couldn't see anymore.

Her whole body glistening with sweat, the black woman licked my body. Gazing into my eyes, she sucked up the flesh of my thighs with her bacon-smelling tongue. Red, moist eyes. Her big mouth kept laughing and laughing.

Soon I was lying down; Moko, her hands braced on the edge of the bed, shook her butt as Saburō thrust into her. Everyone else was crawling on the floor, moving, shaking, making noises.

I noticed that my heart was beating terribly slowly. As if matching its beat, the black woman squeezed my pulsing prick. It was as if only my heart and my cock were attached to each other and working, as if all my other organs had melted.

The black woman sat on top of me. At the same time her hips began to swivel at tremendous speed. She turned her face to the ceiling, let out a Tarzan yell, panted like a black javelin thrower I'd seen in an Olympic film; she braced the grayish soles of her feet on the mattress, thrust her long hands under my hips and held tight. I shouted, felt torn apart. I tried to pull away, but the black woman's body was hard and slippery as greased steel. Pain mixed with pleasure drilled through my lower body and swirled up to my head. My toes were hot enough to melt. My shoulders began to shake, maybe I was going to start yelling. The back of my throat was blocked by something like the soup Jamaicans make with blood and grease, I wanted to spit it up. The black woman took deep breaths, felt my shaft to make sure it was deep inside her, grinned, and took a puff on a very long black cigarette.

She put the perfumed cigarette in my mouth, asked me quickly something I didn't understand, and when I nodded she put her face to mine and sucked my saliva, then began to swivel her hips. Slippery juices streamed from her crotch, wetting my thighs and belly. The speed of her twisting slowly increased. I moaned, getting into it. As I screwed both eyes shut, emptied my head, and put my strength into my feet, keen sensations raced around my body along with my blood and concentrated in my temples. Once the sensations formed and clung to my body, they didn't leave. The thin flesh behind my temples sizzled like skin burned by a firecracker. As I noticed this burn and the feeling became centered there, I somehow believed I had become just one huge penis. Or was I a miniature man who could crawl up inside women and pleasure them with his writhing? I tried to grip the black woman's shoulders. Without slackening the speed of her hips, she leaned forward and bit my nipples until blood came.

Singing a song, Jackson straddled my face. Hey, baby, he said, lightly swatting my cheek. I thought his swollen asshole was like a strawberry. Sweat from his thick chest dripped onto my face, the smell strengthened the stimulus from the black woman's hips. Hey, Ryū, you're just a doll, you're just our little yellow doll, we could stop winding you up and finish you off, y'know, Jackson crooned, and the black woman laughed so loudly I wanted to cover my ears. Her loud voice might have been a broken radio. She laughed without stopping the movement of her hips, and her saliva dribbled onto my belly. She tongue-kissed Jackson. Like a dying fish, my cock jumped inside her. My body seemed powder dry from her heat. Jackson thrust his hot prick into my dry mouth, a hot stone burning my tongue. As he rubbed it around my tongue, he and the black woman chanted something like a spell. It wasn't English, I couldn't understand it. It was like a sutra with a conga rhythm. When my cock twitched and I was almost ready to come, the black woman raised her hips, thrust her hand under my buttocks, pinched me, and jabbed a finger hard into my asshole. When she noticed the tears filling my eyes, she forced her finger in even deeper and twisted it around. There was a whitish tattoo on each of her thighs, a crude picture of a grinning Christ.

She squeezed my throbbing cock, then plunged it into her mouth until her lips almost touched my belly. She licked all around, nipped, then stroked the tip with her rough pointed tongue, just like a cat's. Whenever I was on the verge of coming, she pulled her tongue away. Her buttocks, slippery, shiny with sweat, faced me. They seemed spread almost wide enough to tear apart. I stretched out a hand and dug my nails into one side as hard as I could. The black woman panted and slowly moved her butt from side to side. The fat white woman sat on my feet. Her blackish-red cunt hanging down from under sparse golden down reminded me of a cut-up pig's liver. Jackson seized her huge breasts roughly and pointed to my face. Shaking the breasts that lay on her white belly, she peered into my face, touched my lips split by Jackson's prick, and laughed Pretty in a soft voice. She took one of my legs and rubbed it against her sticky pig liver. My toes were moved around—it felt so bad I could hardly stand it—the white woman smelled just like rotten crab meat and I wanted to throw up. My throat convulsed and I nipped Jackson's prick slightly; he yelled terribly, pulled out, and struck me hard on the cheek. The white woman laughed at my bleeding nose, Gee that's awful; she rubbed her crotch even harder against my feet. The black woman licked up my blood. She smiled gently at me like a battlefield nurse and whispered in my ear Pretty soon we'll have you shoot off, we'll make you come. My right foot began to disappear into the white woman's huge cunt. Again Jackson thrust his prick into my cut mouth. I desperately fought down my nausea. Stimulated by my slippery, bloody tongue, Jackson shot his warm wad. The sticky stuff blocked my throat. I heaved pinkish fluid, mixed with blood, and yelled to the black woman, Make me come!

Damp air stroked my face. Poplar leaves rustled and rain fell slowly. There was the smell of cold wet grass and concrete.

Falling rain lit up by headlights looked like silver needles.

Kei and Reiko had gone with the blacks to a club on the Base. The black woman—she was a dancer named Rudianna—had tried to get me to go to her place.

The silver needles gradually became thicker, the puddles reflecting the tall lights in the hospital garden widened. The wind made ripples on the puddles and the bands of weak light moved complexly.

A hard-shelled insect was knocked off the trunk of a poplar by the wind-blown rain; upside down in flowing water, it tried to swim. I wondered if that kind of beetle had a nest to go back to.

Its black body, glistening in the light, could at first be mistaken for a piece of glass. The beetle managed to climb up on a rock and decided which way to go. Perhaps thinking itself safe, it climbed down on a clump of grass, but this was immediately mowed down by a rivulet of flowing rainwater and the insect was swallowed up.

The rain made a variety of sounds in different places. As it was sucked down into the grass and pebbles and earth, it sounded like tiny musical instruments. The tinkle of a toy piano, small enough to hold on the palm of the hand, blended with the ringing in my ears, the aftermath of the heroin.

A woman was running in the street. She splashed along barefoot, holding her shoes. Maybe because her wet skirt tended to cling to her body, she held the hem wide and avoided the water thrown up by cars.

Lightning flashed, the rain fell harder. My pulse was terribly slow, my body very cold.

The dried fir tree on the veranda had been bought by Lilly last Christmas. The last silver star was gone from the top. Kei had said she'd used it to dance with. She'd said she'd trimmed the tips so they wouldn't prick her thighs and pasted it on when she did the strip.

I was cold; only my feet were hot. Sometimes the heat rose slowly to my head. It was a ball of heat like a peach pit and when it rose, it clawed my heart and stomach and lungs and throat and gums.

The wet scenery outside seemed gentle. Its blurred contours collected raindrops, and voices and the sound of cars had their corners smoothed off by the steadily falling silver needles of rain. The dark outside seemed to suck me up. It was dark and wet like a woman lying down, her strength spent.

When I tossed away my lighted cigarette, it made a little noise and went out before it reached the ground.

"Do you remember that time some feathers were sticking out of the pillow, and after we did it you pulled one out and said, Wow, feathers are so soft, and stroked me behind the ear and on on the chest with it and then threw it on the floor—you remember?"

Lilly had brought along the mescaline. She'd hugged me and asked, What've you been doing, all by yourself? And when I told her I've been watching the rain on the veranda, she talked about the feather.

She lightly nipped my ear, took the blue capsules wrapped in foil from her bag, and put them on the table.

Thunder rumbled and rain was coming in; she told me to close the veranda door.

"Yeah, well, I've just been looking outside. Didn't you look at the rain when you were a kid? Not playing outside, you know, I just used to look out the window at the rain, Lilly, it's really fine."

"Ryū, you're a weird guy, I'm really sorry for you, even if you close your eyes, don't you try and see what comes floating by? I don't really know how to say it, but if you're really honestly having fun, you're not supposed to think and look for things right in the middle of it, am I right?

"You're always trying so hard to see something, just like you're taking notes, like some scholar doing research, right? Or just like a little kid. You really are a little kid, when you're a kid you try to see everything, don't you? Babies look right into the eyes of people they don't know and cry or laugh, but now you just try and look right into people's eyes, you'll go nuts before you know it. Just try it, try looking right into the eyes of people walking past, you'll start feeling funny pretty soon, Ryū, you shouldn't look at things like a baby.''

Lilly's hair was damp. We took one mescaline capsule each, washed down with cold milk.

''I haven't really thought of it like that, you know, I do have a lot of fun—but it's fun looking outside.''

I wiped her body with a towel and hung her wet jacket on a hanger. When I asked, Want me to put on a record? Lilly shook her head and said, Let's have it quiet.

Lilly, I guess you've gone for drives, you know, when you take several hours to go to the sea or to a volcano or something, setting out in the morning when your eyes are still sore, and drinking tea from a thermos at some pretty place along the way, and at noon eating rice balls in a meadow—you know, just an ordinary kind of drive.

And while you're in the car, you think of lots of things, right? When I left home this morning, I couldn't find my camera filter, where's it got to? Or, what was the name of that actress I saw on TV yesterday? Or, my shoelace is ready to break, or I'm really scared of having an accident, or I wonder if I'm not going to grow any taller—you think of a lot of things, right? And then those thoughts and the scenes you see moving by the car pile up on top of each other.

The houses and fields, they slowly come closer and then drop far away behind you, don't they? And that scenery and the stuff inside your head mix together. People waiting at bus stops and a drunk in formal dress staggering along, and an old woman with a cart piled full of oranges, and fields of flowers and harbors and power plants—you see them and then soon you can't see them anymore, so they mix in your head with what you were thinking about before, do you know what I mean? That lost camera filter and the fields of flowers and the power plant all come together. And then I slowly mix them around, just the way I like, the things I see and the things I'm thinking, taking a long time and pulling out dreams and books I've read and memories, to make— how can I say it?—a photo, a scene like a souvenir photo.

And bit by bit I add to this photo the new scenery I keep seeing, and finally in the photo I have people talking and singing and moving around, right? You know, I have them moving around. And then every time, you know, every time, it gets like this huge sort of palace, there's this thing like a palace in my head, with lots of people getting together and doing lots of things.

Then it's really fun to finish this palace and look inside, just like looking down at earth from above the clouds, because there's everything there, everything in the world. All kinds of people talking different languages, and the pillars in the palace are made in lots of different styles, and food from everywhere in the world is all laid out.

It's so much bigger and more detailed than something like a movie set. There're all kinds of people, really all kinds of people. Blind men and beggars and cripples and clowns and dwarfs, generals with gold braid and soldiers smeared with blood, cannibals and blacks in drag and prima donnas and matadors and body-builders, and nomads praying in the desert—they're all there and doing something. And I watch them.

The palace is always by the sea and it's just beautiful, my palace is.

It's like I have my own amusement park and I can go to never-never land whenever I like, I can push a button and watch the models move.

And while I'm enjoying myself like that, the car reaches where it's going to, and while I carry out the luggage and put up the tent and change into my swim trunks and other people talk to me, you know, I'm really having a hard time trying to protect the palace I've made. When other people say Hey, the water's nice here, not polluted, or something like that, it just knocks down my palace—you understand, too, don't you, Lilly?

One time, when I went to a volcano, when I went to a famous live volcano in Kyushu, when I went to the top and saw the dust and ashes spouting out all at once I wanted to blow up my palace. No, when I smelled the sulphur of that volcano, it lit the fuse already attached to the dynamite. A war, you know, Lilly, will finish off the palace. The doctors run around and the soldiers point out roads but its already too late, feet are blown off, since the war's already started it's not as if I had anything to do with it, not as if I started it, and before you know it everything's in ruins.

Because it's a palace I make myself and it doesn't really matter what happens to it, it's always like that, you know, whenever I go on a drive, and looking outside on rainy days helps, too.

Listen, a while back, when I went up to Kawaguchi lake with Jackson and the others, I dropped Acid, and when I tried to make that palace, it didn't turn out to be just a palace but a city, you know, a city.

A city with I don't know how many roads and parks and schools and churches and plazas and broadcasting towers and factories and harbors and stations and markets and zoos and government offices and slaughterhouses. And I even decided on the expression and blood type of every person living in that city.

I keep thinking, won't somebody make a movie like what's inside my head, I'm always thinking that.

A woman falls in love with a married man, he goes off to war and kills a child in a foreign country, that child's mother saves him in a storm without knowing what he's done, a girl is born, she grows up and becomes a whore for a gang, the gang's really cool but a district attorney is shot, and his father was in the

Gestapo during the war, and finally the girl, she's walking down a road lined with trees while a Brahms piece plays in the backgound—I mean, not that kind of movie.

It would be like when, you know, you cut up a big cow and eat a steak just about this big. No, that's hard to understand, but listen, even with a little steak you've still eaten the whole cow, you know. So I'd like to see a movie that cut out a little bit of the palace or the city in my head, like cutting up a cow, I think it really could be done.

I think it would be a movie like an enormous mirror, a huge mirror, reflecting everyone who saw it, I'd really like to see that movie, if there were a movie like that I'd see it for sure.

Lilly said, "And let me tell you what the first scene of that movie would be—a helicopter, you know, would come carrying a statue of Jesus Christ, how about it? O.K.?

"The mesc has gotten to you, too. Hey, Ryū, let's go for a drive, let's go to a volcano, and you'll make up a city again and tell me about it, I'm sure it's raining, in that city. I want to see that city, too, with the thunder rumbling, you know, I'm going!"

I said over and over that it would be dangerous to drive but Lilly wouldn't listen. Seizing the key, she ran out into the whiplike rain.

Neon signs that pierced the eyes and headlights from oncoming cars that split the body in two, trucks that passed with a sound just like the cries of enormous waterfowl, big trees that suddenly stood in our way and abandoned ruined houses beside the road, factories with mysterious machines lined up and flames spouting from smokestacks, the winding road like molten steel flowing from a blast furnace.

The surging dark river crying like a living thing, tall grass beside the road dancing in the wind, a barbed-wire enclosed electric transformer station panting steam, and Lilly laughing, laughing crazily, and me, seeing it all.

Everything glowed with a light of its own.

The rain magnified, amplified everything. The light made shadows stretch blue-white on the white walls of sleeping houses and startled us as if some monster had bared its teeth for an instant.

We must be running under the ground here, in a huge tunnel, here for sure, we can't see the stars and the sewer water's pouring down. And it's so cold, there must have been a rift in the ground, there're only creatures we don't know here.

Aimless weaving and repeated sudden stops—neither of us had any idea where we were going.

Lilly stopped the car in front of the noisy towering transformer station, which floated in the light.

The whirlpools of thick coils were surrounded by a wire fence. We gazed at an iron tower like a sheer cliff.

This must be a courthouse, Lilly said and started to laugh, and looked around the wide, glowing fields surrounding the transformer station. The tomato fields rippling in the wind.

It's just like the sea, she said.

The tomatos were wet and wonderfully red in the darkness. They flashed on and off like the little light bulbs on fir trees or around windows at Christmas time. The numberless trembling red fruits, trailing sparks, were just like fish with luminous teeth swimming in the dark sea.

"What're those?"

"I guess they're tomatos, they sure don't look like tomatos."

"It's just like the sea, a sea in a country we've never been to. Something's floating, in that sea."

"There must be mines laid here, you can't go in, it's protected. You touch one of those, you'll blow up and die, they're protecting the sea."

There was a long, low building beyond the fields. I thought it must be a school or factory.

The lightning flashed and filled the car with white sparks. Lilly screamed.

Her bared legs showed goose bumps, she shook the steering wheel, her teeth chattered.

It's just lightning, calm down, Lilly.

She yelled, What are you talking about, and all at once opened the door. A monster's roar filled the car.

''I'm going into the sea, I can't breathe in here, let go of me, let me go!''

Drenched in a second, Lilly slammed the door behind her. Her hair fluttering, she passed in front of the windshield. Pink smoke rose to the sky from the hood, and steam rose from the road lit by the headlights. Beyond the glass, Lilly shouted something, baring her teeth. Maybe that really was the sea over there. Lilly was a shimmering deep-sea fish.

She beckoned to me. Her gesture and expression were just the the same as a little girl I'd seen once in a dream, chasing a white ball.

The sound of the windshield wipers squeaking against the glass made me think of the giant clams that can seize and dissolve people.

In that closed metal room, the white seats were as soft and slippery as the flesh of a giant clam.

The walls shook and exuded a strong acid, surrounding and dissolving me.

Come quick! You'll melt in there!

Lilly went into the field. Her spread arms were fins, she rippled her body, the raindrops on her were shining scales.

I opened the door.

The wind roared as if the whole earth were shaking.

The tomatos, with no glass between me and them, weren't

red. They were nearly that special orange of the clouds at sunset. A whitish orange flashing through glass vacuum bottles that burns on the retina even when your eyes are closed.

I ran after Lilly. On the tomato leaves brushing my arms grew a light down.

Lilly tore apart a tomato, Hey, Ryū, look, it's just like a light bulb, all lit up. I ran to her, grabbed the tomato, and threw it into the sky.

Get down, Lilly! That's a grenade—get down! Lilly laughed loudly and we fell to the ground together.

It's like we're down in the sea, it's so quiet I'm almost scared. Ryū, I can hear your breathing, and mine, too.

The tomatos looking up from this place were breathing quietly, too. Their breath mixed with ours and moved like mist among the stalks. In the puddly black earth were broken grass stalks, they pricked our skin, and thousands of tiny resting insects. Their breath reached here from deep in the earth.

Look, that must be a school, I can see a pool, Lilly said.

The ash-gray building drew in sound and moisture and pulled us toward it. That school building floating in the darkness was like the golden exit at the end of a long cave. Dragging our bodies, heavy with mud, and trampling on overripe fallen tomatos, we crossed the field.

When we got out of the wind and rain under the eaves of the school building, we felt as if we were in the shadow of a dirigible floating in the sky. It was too quiet, and the cold attacked us.

At the edge of the wide grounds was a pool, and around it flowers were planted. Like the eruptions on a rotting corpse, like a serum with multiplying cancer cells, the flowers were blooming. Against the background of a wall that rippled like white cloth, they scattered on the ground or suddenly danced up in the wind.

I'm cold, as if I were dead, Lilly said.

She was shaking and pulled me back toward the car. The classrooms seen through the windows seemed ready to devour us. The desks and chairs in regular rows reminded me of a mass grave for unknown soldiers. Lilly was trying to escape the silence.

Running with all my might, I cut across the grounds. Lilly yelled after me.

Come back, I'm begging you, you just can't go!

I struggled up to the wire fence around the pool, and started climbing it. On the water below, ripples and counterripples blended into each other, looking just like a TV screen after all the day's broadcasting has ended. The water glittered, reflecting the lightning.

Do you know what you're doing? Come back, you'll die, you'll end up dead!

Her arms hugging her body, her legs twisted around each other, Lilly was yelling in the middle of the grounds.

Tense as a deserter from the army, I dropped down beside the pool. Thousands of ripples were forming constantly, the water looked like translucent jelly—I hurled myself in.

Lightning lit up the inside of Lilly's hands on the steering wheel. Blue lines lay buried in the transparent skin, water drops rolled down her muddy arms. On the road like a twisted metal tube, the car ran along beside the barbed wire enclosure around the Base.

"Hey, I completely forgot."

"What?" she asked.

"In the city in my head I forgot to put in an airport."

Strands of Lilly's mud-smeared hair clung together. Her face was pale, tiny veins pulsed in her neck, her shoulders were covered with goose pimples.

I saw the water drops rolling down the windshield as being

just like the round beetles of summer. Just like the little beetles that reflect the whole forest on their rounded backs.

Lilly kept mixing up the accelerator and the brake, her white legs stretched out stiffly and she shook her head violently to clear it.

"Hey, the city's just about done, but it's a city under the sea. So what'll I do about the airport, don't you have some idea, Lilly?"

"Look, cut out the stupid talk, I'm scared, we've got to get back."

"You should have washed off the mud, too, Lilly, won't it feel bad when it dries? It was beautiful in the pool, the water was glowing. That's when I decided to make it an undersea city, you know."

"I said cut it out! Hey Ryū, tell me where we are now. I don't know where we're going, I can't see too well, hey, pull yourself together. We might die, dying is all I've been thinking about. Where are we, Ryū, tell me where we are!"

Suddenly a metallic orange light flashed as if exploding in the car, Lilly wailed like a siren and let go of the steering wheel.

At once I pulled the hand brake and the squealing car slid to the side, mauled the barbed-wire enclosure, hit a light pole, and stopped.

A-ah, it's a plane, look, it's a plane!

The runway swarmed with all kinds of light.

A sheaf of searchlights revolved, the windows of buildings twinkled, guide lights along empty spaces flashed.

The deafening roar of the sparkling, polished jet standing beside the runway shook everything around.

There were three searchlights on a tall tower. After their cylinders of light passed us—necks of dinosaurs—the distant mountains shone. One lump of rain over there, cut away by the light, congealed into a sparkling silver room. The strongest searchlight turned slowly, lighting fixed areas, lighting another runway a short distance from us. We had lost our willpower in the shock of impact. Like cheap robots wound up and set to walk a certain direction, we got out of the car and walked toward the runway, closer to the jet roar shaking the ground.

Now the light picked out the sides of the mountains in the opposite direction. Its huge sweeping orange circle peeled off the night, easily peeled off the night stuck to and wrapped around things.

Lilly took off her shoes. She threw the muddy shoes against the barbed-wire enclosure. The light soon swept through the woods alongside it. Sleeping birds were startled into flight.

It's going to be soon, Ryū, I'm scared, it's going to be soon.

The barbed wire flared gold, and the light seen up close was like a red-hot iron bar. The circle of light stopped nearby. Steam rose from the earth. The earth and grass and runway turned the white of molten glass.

First Lilly entered the whiteness. Then I did. For a moment we couldn't hear anything. In a few seconds unbearable pain struck our ears. It was as if they had been pierced with hot needles. Lilly clutched hers and fell backward. My chest was filled with the odor of burning.

The rain stabbed us, the way skinned meat hung in a freezer is speared with iron rods.

Lilly was searching for something on the ground. Like a near-sighted soldier who'd lost his glasses on the battlefield, she felt around frantically.

What was she looking for?

The thick drooping clouds, the ceaseless rain, the grass where the insects slept, the whole ash-gray Base, the wet runway reflecting the Base, and the air moving like waves—all were controlled by the jet spouting its enormous flames.

It started down the runway slowly. The earth shook. The huge silvery metal gradually picked up speed. Its high-pitched whine seared the air. Close in front of us, four enormous tube-shaped engines spouted blue flame. The stench of heavy oil and the violent blast of air blew me off my feet.

My face distorted, I hit the ground. My clouded eyes tried desperately to see. As I was thinking the white belly of the plane had just floated off the ground, before I knew it, it was sucked toward the clouds.

Lilly was looking at me. There was white froth between her teeth, and a trickle of blood as if she'd bitten the inside of her mouth.

Hey, Ryū, what about the city?

The plane came to rest in the middle of the sky.

It seemed to have stopped, a toy hanging by a wire from the ceiling of a department store. I thought we were the ones moving away with tremendous force. I thought the earth spreading away from our feet and the grass and the runway had all plunged downward.

Hey, Ryū, what about the city? Lilly asked, lying sprawled on her back on the runway.

She took lipstick from her pocket, tore off her clothes and smeared it on her body, laughingly drawing red lines on her belly, chest, neck.

I realized that my head was full of nothing but the stench of heavy oil. There was nothing like a city anywhere.

Lilly drew a design on her face with lipstick, becoming one of the African women who dance crazily at festivals.

Hey, Ryū, kill me. Something's weird, Ryū, I want you to kill me, Lilly called, tears in her eyes. I threw myself off the runway. My body was clawed by the wire. The barbs bit into the flesh of my shoulder. I thought I wanted a hole opened in me. I wanted to be free of the oil stench, that was all I thought. Concentrating on that I forgot where I was. Groveling on the ground, Lilly called to me. Her legs flung out, naked, bound redly to the ground, she kept saying, Kill me! I went close to her. Her body shaking violently, she sobbed aloud.

Kill me quick, kill me quick! I touched her red-striped neck.

Then one side of the sky lit up.

For an instant the blue-white flash made everything transparent. Lilly's body and my arms and the Base and the mountains and the cloudy sky were transparent. And then I discovered a single curved line running through the transparency there. It had a shape I'd never seen before, a white curving, a white curving that made splendid arcs.

Ryū, you know you're a baby? You're just a baby after all.

I took my hand from Lilly's neck, and scooped the white froth from her mouth with my tongue. She took off my clothes and embraced me.

Oil flowing from somewhere separated around our bodies; it was colored like a rainbow.

Early in the morning the rain let up. The kitchen window and glass sliding doors shone like sheets of silver.

While I was breathing in the scents of the warming air and fixing coffee, the outside door suddenly opened. There stood three cops, their thick chests wrapped in sweaty-smelling uniforms, white braid hanging from their shoulders. Startled, I spilled the sugar on the floor. One of the younger cops asked me, ''What're you kids up to in here?''

I just stood there without answering, and the two cops in front pushed me aside and came into the room. Ignoring Kei and Reiko lying there, they stood with folded arms before the veranda door, then violently yanked the curtain open.

At that sound and the strong light pouring in, Kei leaped to her feet. With the light behind them, the cops looked very big.

The older fat officer left standing in the entranceway nudged aside the shoes scattered there with his foot and slowly entered the room.

''Well, we don't have a warrant, but you're not going to make any fuss about that, are you? Is this your place? Is it?'' He seized my arm and checked it for needle marks.

''You're in college?'' The fat officer's fingers were short and his nails were dirty. Although he wasn't holding me very hard, I couldn't shake free. I gazed at the hand, washed with morning sunlight, of the officer who had caught me so casually, as if I had never seen a hand before.

The other people in the room, all almost naked, were hurrying to put on their clothes. The two young cops were whispering together. From where I stood I could hear words like "pigsty" and "marijuana."

"Get dressed fast, hey you, put on some slacks."

Kei, still just in her panties, pouted and glared at the fat officer. Yoshiyama and Kazuo stood by the window, their faces frozen. As they rubbed their eyes, one cop ordered them to turn off the noisy radio. By the wall, Reiko clawed through her handbag, found her hairbrush and straightened her hair. The cop with glasses picked up her purse and dumped its contents out on the table.

"Hey, what are you doing, quit it," Reiko protested in a faint voice, but the cop just snorted and ignored her.

Moko, naked, was still lying flat on her stomach on the bed, making no effort to get up, her sweaty flanks exposed to the light. The young cops stared at the black hair sticking out from between her buttocks. I went over and shook her shoulder, saying, Get up, and covered her with the blanket.

"You, get on some slacks, what are you looking at me like that for, huh?" Kei muttered something and turned away, but Kazuo tossed her some jeans and she pulled them on, clicking her tongue. Her throat trembled.

Hands on their hips, the three looked around the room and checked the ashtray. Moko finally opened her eyes and mumbled Huh? What? Who are these guys? The cops snickered.

"Hey, you kids, you've got it too much your own way, it bothers us, all of you lying around naked in the daytime, maybe it doesn't matter to you, but some people—not like you punks— know how it is to feel ashamed."

The older officer opened the veranda window, letting out a shower of dust.

The morning town seemed too bright to make out details. The bumpers of cars passing on the road glinted and I felt sick.

The cops seemed one whole size larger than any of the rest of us in the room.

"Uh, is it O.K. if I smoke?" Kazuo asked, but the cop with glasses said Forget it, took the cigarette from between his fingers, and put it back in the pack. Reiko helped Moko put on some underwear. Very pale and shaking, Moko hooked on her bra.

Fighting my rising nausea, I asked, "Has there been some trouble?"

The three looked at each other and laughed loudly.

"Trouble? Hey, that's good, coming from you! Listen, you just don't show your butts in front of other people, maybe you don't know it, but you shouldn't act like dogs.

"You kids got families? They don't say anything about the way you carry on? They don't care, huh? We know how you swap each other around. Hey you, you'd probably do it with your own daddy, huh? I mean you!"

He turned and spoke loudly to Kei. Her eyes brimmed tears.

"Hey, you little bitch, did I make you feel bad?"

Moko kept on trembling and didn't seem likely to stop, so Reiko buttoned her shirt for her.

Kei started for the kitchen, but the fat officer grabbed her arm and held her back.

After Yoshiyama, the oldest, had turned in the standard apology forms at the dusty smelling police station, without going back to the apartment we set out to hear a performance by the Bar Kays at the Hibiya Park open-air concert stage. We were all tired from lack of sleep. No one spoke on the train.

"Yeah, it was real lucky they didn't find that hash, Ryū. Even though it was right there in front of them, they just didn't know it. It was real lucky they were fuzz from the substation and not security cops, real lucky," Yoshiyama sneered as we got off the train. Kei made a disgusted face and spat on the platform. In the station washroom Moko passed out Nibrole pills to everyone.

Crunching his pill, Kazuo asked Reiko, "Hey, what were you talking about with that young cop, out there in the hall?"

"He told me he's a Led Zeppelin fan. He'd been to a design school, he was an O.K. guy."

"Is that right? You should have told him about somebody stealing my strobe."

I crunched a pill, too.

When we came in sight of the woods around the place, everybody was already stoned. From the outdoor theater in the woods, the rock music sounded loud enough to shake the leaves. Children with roller skates on their feet were looking through the wire fence around the place at the long-haired people leaping on the stage. A couple sitting on a bench saw Yoshiyama's rubber sandals and chuckled to each other. A young mother holding her baby frowned after us. Some little girls, running along holding big balloons, stopped short when they were startled by the sudden shriek of the vocals. One let go of her ballon and looked ready to cry. The big red balloon danced slowly upward.

"Hey, man, no bread," Yoshiyama said to me as I bought a ticket at the entrance. Moko said she had a friend working with the concert and started toward the stage. Kei bought her own ticket and hurried on in.

When I said, I don't have enough for two, he said, So I'll climb over the fence again, and started toward the back, inviting Kazuo, who didn't have any money either, to come with him.

"I wonder if they'll be O.K.," I said, but Reiko didn't seem to hear me because of the tremendous volume of the guitar solo. All kinds of amps and speakers were lined up on the stage, just like a display of toy blocks. A girl in a green lamé jump suit was singing "Me and Bobby Magee," though you couldn't make out the words. She jerked her body up every time the big glittering cymbals clashed. The people in the front rows were clapping their hands and dancing, their mouths open. The noise whirled around the tiers of seats and rose to the sky. Every time the guitarist swung down his right hand, my ears tingled. The individual sounds massed together, split the earth. I walked around the part of the fan-shaped amphitheater farthest from the stage, along the last row of seats, thinking it was just like summer, when all the cicadas are buzzing together in a forest during the morning. Someone shook a nylon glue-sniffing bag, clouded with white vapor, someone put an arm around the shoulders of a girl laughing with her mouth wide open, someone wore a T-shirt with a picture of Jimi Hendrix on it, all kinds of shoes pounded on the earth. Leather *zori*, sandals with leather thongs wound around the ankles, silver vinyl boots with spurs, bare feet, enameled high heels, basket shoes—and all shades of lipstick, nail polish, eye shadow, hair, and rouge shook in time to the music in one great commotion. Beer foamed, overflowed, cola bottles broke, cigarette smoke rose steadily, sweat flowed down the face of a foreign girl with a diamond set in her forehead, a bearded guy shook a rolled-up green scarf, standing up on a chair and jerking his shoulders. A girl with a feather in her hat spat out saliva, a girl with green-rimmed sunglasses, lips stretched wide, bit the insides of her cheeks. She clasped her hands behind her and jerked her hips. Her long dirty skirt rippled like waves. The movement of the air seemed focused in her as she swayed back and forth.

"Hey, Ryū, isn't it Ryū?"

The guy who spoke to me had spread some black felt on the ground beside the water fountain at a corner by the path, and lined up on it metal handicrafts, pins and necklaces dangling animal fangs and bones, Indian incense, and pamphlets about yoga and drugs.

"What's up? You've gone into business?"

This guy, he was nicknamed Male, grinned at me as I came over, spread and circled those hands that had always put on Pink Floyd records when we were staying over at some coffee shop, a long time ago.

"Naw, I'm just helping out a friend," he said, shaking his head. He was thin, his toes were black with dirt, one of his front teeth was broken.

"It's a real bummer, this kind of crummy music is all over these days, and before this there were those fag singers, Julie or somebody, I threw a rock at them. You're over by the Yokota Base, right? How is it, any fun?"

"Yeah, well, because there're black guys, when there're blacks around it's cool, because they're really something else, blowing grass and pouring down vodka and then while they're stoned playing the best kind of sax, you know, really something else."

Just in front of the stage Moko was dancing, almost naked. Two cameramen clicked their shutters at her. A guy who'd thrown some burning paper among the seats was surrounded and taken out by several guards. A little guy holding a glue-sniffing bag staggered up onto the stage and hugged the girl singer from behind. Three of the people in charge tried to pull him off her. He clutched the waist of her lamé jump suit and made a grab for the mike. Angry, the bass guitarist pounded his back with a mike stand. The little guy leaned backward, clutching the small of his back, seemed about to fall, then he was pushed off into the front seats by the bass guitarist. The people dancing there yelled and jumped aside. The little guy had fallen headfirst, still holding the glue bag; he was dragged out by both arms by guards.

"Ryū, do you remember Meg? You know, the girl who came to us in Kyoto and wanted to play organ in our band? With the big eyes, right, the one who told that whopper about her taking off from the arts college," Male said, pulling a cigarette from my shirt pocket and lighting it. Smoke seeped out from the gap in his teeth.

"Sure I remember."

"She came to Tokyo, to my place, I wanted to get in touch with you too but didn't know your address. Because she was saying she wanted to see you, too, you know, it must have been around the time right after you moved."

"Is that so? I really wanted to see her, too."

"We lived together for a while. She was a good kid, Ryū, a really good kid. Yeah, she was sweet, she felt sorry for this rabbit that hadn't been sold and swapped her watch for it. She was a rich kid, the watch was an Omega, for this lousy rabbit, really too much, but she was that kind of girl."

"She's still around?"

Without answering, Male pulled up his trouser leg to bare the left calf. Pink burn scars puckered the skin all the way up.

"What's that, you got burned? What happened? That's really bad."

"Yeah, it's bad all right, we were stoned and dancing around, you know, in my room. Her skirt caught fire from my gas stove, you know, a long skirt. It really burned fast, just roared up in a second and you couldn't even see her face."

He brushed back his trailing hair with one finger and stubbed out the cigarette on the bottom of his sandal.

"She was burned black, a charred body is one thing you don't ever want to see, you know, it's really bad. Her dad came over right away, and how old do you think she was really? She was fifteen, just fifteen, I was really freaked to hear she'd been fifteen."

He pulled gum from his pocket and put some in his broken-toothed mouth. I didn't want any and waved it aside.

"If I'd known how old she was at the beginning, I would've sent her back to Kyoto. She said she was twenty-one, she acted like it, so I believed her, really I did."

Then Male said he might be going back to the country, so I should come visit him.

"I'm always remembering how her face looked then, I didn't do her dad any favor either, and I'm never going to take anything like Hyminal again."

"Was your piano O.K.?"

"In the fire? The only thing that burned was her, you know, the piano wasn't even scorched."

"But you're not playing it?"

"Naw, I'm playing it all right, I'm still playing, but what about you, Ryū?"

"I've gotten rusty."

Male stood up and went to buy two cokes. He offered me some leftover popcorn. A warm breeze blew, now and then.

The bubbles pricked my throat, numb from the Nibrole. On the black felt, a little mirror with a decorated edge reflected my yellowed eyes.

"You know how I used to play The Doors' 'Crystal Ship'?

"Now when I hear that I could cry, when I hear that piano it's just like I'm playing it myself, I just can't stand it. Maybe pretty soon I won't be able to stand hearing anything, they're all so damn nostalgic. I'm just fed up, what about you, Ryū? Because pretty soon we'll both be twenty, right? I don't want to end up like Meg, I don't ever want to see anybody like that again."

"You'll go back to playing Schumann?"

"I don't mean that, you know, but I sure want to get out of this lousy life-style—I just don't know what to do."

Grade-school kids in black uniforms were passing by in three lines on the path below. A woman with a guide flag who looked like a teacher was telling them something in a loud voice. One little girl stopped and stared at me and Male leaning against the wire fence, both long haired and tired looking. She wore a red hat and she gazed at us while her friends jostled past her. Her head was tapped by the teacher and so she started off again in a fluster. She ran to catch up with the line, her white rucksack shaking. Before she was out of sight, she turned back just once to look at us again.

"A school trip," I muttered.

Male spat out the gum and laughed, "Do school kids go on trips?"

"Hey, Male, what happened to the rabbit?"

'The rabbit? I kept it awhile but it gave me bad vibes, and there's no one else who'd take it."

"Maybe I would."

"Huh? Too late, I ate it."

"Ate it?"

"Yeah, I asked the neighborhood butcher to fix it for me, but it was a baby rabbit and didn't have much meat on it. I poured on ketchup, you know, but it was kind of tough."

"You ate it, huh?"

The noise from the huge speakers seemed to have nothing to do with the people moving on the stage.

It seemed that noise had been going on from the beginning of time, and monkeys wearing makeup were dancing to it.

Dripping sweat, Moko came up, glanced at Male, hugged me.

"Yoshiyama's calling for you, over there. Kazuo got beat up by the guards and he's hurt."

Male sat down again in front of the black felt. "Hey, Male, tell me when you're going back to the country."

I tossed him a pack of Kools.

"Yeah, take care of yourself." He tossed me a pin made of translucent shell. "There you are, Ryū, that's a crystal ship."

"Hey, Moko, is it really fun, getting all in a sweat dancing to this kind of band?"

"What are you talking about? Don't you just lose out if you don't have a good time?"

Sucking noisily on a joint sopping wet with saliva, Yoshiyama beckoned to us.

"That idiot Kazuo tried to climb the fence right while a guard was watching him. When he tried to get away, he got it on the leg. Too bad. Shit, that guard was a real bastard. Had a bat."

"Somebody took him to the hospital?"

"Yeah, Kei and Reiko, Reiko said she'd go back to her place for a little, and Kei was supposed to take Kazuo back to his apartment. But it really gets to me, really makes me mad."

Yoshiyama passed the joint to the girl with heavy makeup next to him. She had high cheekbones and a lot of green stuff smeared heavily around her eyes. "Hey, what's this?" she asked. The guy holding her hand said into her ear, "You dumb chick, that's marijuana." "Gee, thanks," she said, flashing her eyes. She and her guy sucked on the joint noisily.

Moko swallowed two more Nibrole pills at the water fountain. She was sticky with sweat and her hot pants cut into her stomach and her sides heaved. A cameraman wearing an armband snapped her as she came over to hug me. I pried her arm from around my neck and pulled away.

"Hey, Moko, you can go and dance some more if you want to."

"Huh? Even after I gave you a whiff of my Dior? I hate you, Ryū, you bring me down."

She stuck out her tongue and staggered back to join the dancers. As she leaped her breasts shook, one of them had a freckle on it.

Yoshiyama came running and shouted in my ear, "We've caught the bastard who got Kazuo."

In the dim public toilet was a guard with a shaved head. A half-naked, mixed-blood hippie had the man's arms pinioned, while another guy gagged him tightly with a leather thong. The walls were filthy with graffiti and spider webs and the smell of piss stabbed my nose. Flies buzzed around the broken windows.

As the guard twisted and beat his feet against the floor, Yoshiyama drove an elbow into his belly.

"Hey, you stand watch for us," he said to me.

Once more Yoshiyama buried his elbow almost halfway into the pit of the man's stomach, so that he spewed. From the corner of his mouth, held in a straight line by the leather thong, the yellow stuff dribbled over the back of his neck, soiling his Mickey Mouse T-shirt. His eyes tightly shut, he fought against the pain. The vomit came out again and again, catching on his thick belt, dripping in to soil the inside of his trousers. The well-muscled hippie said to Yoshiyama, "Let me have him for a minute," got in front of the groaning guard, and whipped an open hand across his drooping face. The blow jerked the guard's face to one side, almost hard enough to tear it off. Fresh blood splattered out, I thought a tooth must have been broken. The man fainted and slithered out flat on the floor. The hippie was terribly drunk or stoned on something; his red eyes flashing, he shook off Yoshiyama when he tried to hold him back and then he broke the guard's left arm. A dry sound like a stick snapping. The man groaned and raised his face. His eyes opened wide when he saw his limply dangling arm, and he rolled on the slimy concrete. He turned over once, twice, slowly. The hippie wiped his own hands on a handkerchief, then stuffed the bloody cloth into the mouth of the groaning man. Between the guitar chords that blasted my ears, I could hear the man's panting even from where I stood. When Yoshiyama and the others went out he stopped rolling and tried to crawl forward, his right hand groping on the floor.

"Hey, Ryū, we're leaving."

The blood smeared and dripping over the lower half of his face was a black mask. The veins in his forehead bulging, he tried to pull himself along by his elbows. Perhaps seized by some fresh pain, he mumbled, lay on his side, his feet trembled. His vomit-covered belly heaved up and down.

The inside of the train glittered. Full of the train's roar and the smell of liquor, my chest felt queasy. Yoshiyama wandered around, stoned on Nibrole and red-eyed, and Moko was sitting on the floor by the door. In the station we'd each crunched two more Nibrole pills. Hanging onto the pole, I stood next to Moko. Yoshiyama held his chest and puked, then watched vacantly as other passengers hurried to move away. The sour smell floated to us. Yoshiyama wiped his mouth with a newspaper taken from the overhead rack. With the vibrations of the train, only the liquid spread out from the layer of vomit on the floor. No more passengers got on our car at the stops. Bastards, Yoshiyama muttered, and slammed his hand against the window. My head felt heavy and when I relaxed my grip on the pole I almost fell. Moko raised her head and held my hand, but my senses were so dulled I didn't feel as if it were another person's hand touching me.

"Hey, Ryū, I'm tired enough to die."

Moko kept saying we should go home by taxi. At one side of the car Yoshiyama stood in front of a woman bent over reading a book. Noticing the spittle trailing from his lips, she tried to get away. Yoshiyama yelled, seized her arm, spun her around and hugged her. Her thin blouse tore. Her shriek rang out higher than the screech of the wheels. Passengers escaped to the adjoining cars. The woman dropped her book, and the contents of her handbag scattered on the floor. Moko made a face of disgust in that direction and mumbled, her eyes sleepy, I'm hungry.

Ryū, wouldn't you like a pizza, an anchovy pizza, with lots of tabasco sauce, so hot it prickles your tongue, wouldn't you like one?

The woman pushed Yoshiyama away and ran toward us. Her chin thrust out, she avoided the vomit on the floor and held her bared chest. I tripped her. Then I pulled her to her feet and tried to tongue-kiss her. She clamped her teeth together, shook her head, and tried to pull away.

Bastards, Yoshiyama said in a low voice to the passengers near us. On the other side of the glass, people were looking at us as if peering into a cage at the zoo.

As the train pulled into the next station, we spit at the woman and ran out onto the platform.

Hey, they're the ones, catch them! A middle-aged man yelled as he leaned out of a train window, his necktie fluttering. Yoshiyama heaved again as he ran. His shirt dripped with it and his rubber sandals rang on the platform. Moko, very pale, carried her sandals and ran barefoot. On the stairs Yoshiyama stumbled and fell. He got cut above one eye on the handrail, and blood streamed out. He coughed and muttered something as he ran on. At the exit gate Moko's arm was seized by a station official but Yoshiyama struck the man's face. We rushed into the crowd in the passageway outside. Moko started to sink down, I scooped her up. My eyes hurt; when I rubbed my temples, tears came. Waves of violent nausea seemed to rise from the tiled floor of the passageway, and I clamped my hand over my mouth.

Moko's legs got tangled up as she walked; the smell of the blacks that had clung to her until this morning was now all gone.

Puddles still stood in the garden of the general hospital. Avoiding the tire tracks in the mud, a child ran carrying a bundle of newspapers.

A bird was calling somewhere, but I couldn't see it.

Last night when I'd reached my room, I'd smelled the pineapple and thrown up violently.

When I'd sucked the lips of the woman on the train, her eyes had looked strange. I wondered what her expression had been.

Birds danced down into the apartment garden. The American couple living on the first floor had thrown some bread crumbs out. Looking around nervously, the birds pecked and swallowed quickly. The crumbs had fallen among the pebbles but the birds picked them out skillfully.

A cleaning woman with a cloth wrapped around her head had passed quite near, going toward the hospital, but the birds didn't fly away.

I couldn't see their eyes from where I was. I like birds' eyes with their round borders. These birds were gray with red feathers like crowns on their heads.

I decided to give the pineapple to the birds.

Light cut through the clouds in the east. The air touched by it looked milky. When the first-floor veranda door rattled open, the birds quickly flew up and away.

I went back inside my room and got the pineapple.

"Uh, I thought I'd give this to the birds," I said to the woman who stuck her head out. She seemed friendly. Pointing to the roots of the poplar, she told me, "If you put it there, they can get at it pretty well."

The pineapple I threw down was smashed out of shape when it landed, but still it rolled slowly to a stop beside the poplar. The sound of the pineapple hitting the ground reminded me of the beating in the public toilet yesterday.

The American woman set out for a walk with her poodle. She saw the pineapple and looked up at me, shading her eyes with her hand, I guess because of the light, and she nodded and chuckled, saying I think the birds'll be glad.

"Hey, Okinawa, where'd you go the other night? I was worried about you."

"This guy, he went to a hotel, all alone in this place for couples," Reiko answered. "And, it's awful, well, he looks like this and they were suspicious about him, you know, and he just cut out through a window, wouldn't think of paying. Of course it would've been my money, but that doesn't matter."

That afternoon, Reiko had come over with Okinawa. He was drunk again and really stank, so I said, Let's get you shot up pretty soon and forced him into the bathtub.

Reiko whispered in my ear, Don't tell Okinawa about that stuff with Saburō and the others, because he'd kill me, O.K.? When I laughed and nodded, she took off her clothes and went into the bathroom herself.

Yoshiyama was mad because Kei hadn't come back last night. He hadn't even looked interested when Okinawa showed him the new Doors' record he'd brought.

We could hear Reiko's moans from the bathroom. Looking disgusted, Moko said, "Ryū, put on some music, I'm sick of just fucking, I think there must be something else, I mean, some other ways to have fun."

As I lowered the needle on The Doors' record, Kazuo showed up, limping, with Kei holding him up by the shoulder. We've come to get a souvenir from the party—you got anything? They were both already stoned on Nibrole and they tongue-kissed right there in front of Yoshiyama.

Even while their lips were together, they looked at him as if they could hardly keep from laughing.

Yoshiyama suddenly grabbed Moko, who was lying next to him on the bed reading a magazine, and tried to kiss her. What are you doing, cut it out, in broad daylight, too! That's all you know how to do, Moko yelled and pushed him away. Yoshiyama glared at Kei, who was laughing at the scene. Tossing the magazine on the rug, Moko said, Ryū, I'm going home, I'm sick and tired of this. She pulled on the velvet dress she'd worn when she'd come.

"Kei, where'd you stay last night?" Yoshiyama asked, getting up off the bed.

"Kazuo's place."

"Was Reiko with you?"

"Reiko went to a hotel with Okinawa, a place called the Shin Okubo Love Palace, she said all the ceilings there are made of mirrors."

"You screwed Kazuo?"

Moko shook her head as she listened to them talking. She quickly put on some makeup, fixed her hair, and tapped me on the shoulder. "Give me some hash, Ryū."

"Can ya really say that kind of thing, with everybody listening in?"

"Yeah, don't talk that way, Yoshiyama, didn't she just come along with me because I got hurt? Don't talk funny in front of everybody," Kazuo sneered, then asked me, "Didn't that strobe turn up?"

When I shook my head, he bent down to stroke the bandage around his ankle and muttered, "It cost me ¥20,000 and I'd just bought it, too."

"Hey, Ryū, walk me to the station," Moko said, slipping on her shoes by the door and looking in the mirror to straighten her hat.

"Hey, Moko, you're leaving?" asked Reiko, a towel wrapped around her body, as she drank a coke from the refrigerator.

On the way to the station Moko begged me to buy her a girls' magazine and some cigarettes. The girl from the sales stand, sprinkling water on the sidewalk, recognized me and said, Hey, that's nice, you're on a date. Her bright cream-colored slacks fit tightly, I could see the line of her panties. As she wiped her wet hands on her apron and handed me the cigarettes, she glanced at Moko's red-enameled toenails.

"Does your ass still hurt?" I asked Moko.

"Well, a little when I go to the can, but that guy Jackson is real sweet, he brought me this scarf from the shop at the Base, it's Lanvin."

"You'd do it again? Me, I'm really worn out."

"Yeah, well, it did get kind of rough, but if there's another party I guess I'd go, there aren't really many times you can have fun, are there? When nothing's fun anymore, I'll just get married."

"Huh? You plan to get married?"

"Sure, of course, you thought I didn't?"

A truck made a wild right turn at the intersection, and dust whirled up around us. Fine sand had gotten into my eyes and mouth. I spit it out. Damn driver, muttered the postman who'd gotten off his bicycle and was rubbing his eyes.

"Hey, Ryū, it's about Yoshiyama, keep an eye on him, because he beats up Kei a lot. When he gets drunk he's really mean, kicking her and stuff. Talk to him about it, O.K.?"

"He really means it? He doesn't really mean it, does he?"

"What are you talking about? One time she got a tooth broken. I don't know about that Yoshiyama, because he's like a different guy when he's drunk. Anyway, watch out for him."

"Are your folks O.K., Moko?"

"Yeah, well, my dad's been kind of sick, but my brother—hey, don't you know about him, Ryū?—he's just too straight. That's why I've ended up like this, but these days they're kind of resigned about it, you know, and when I said my photo's in *An-An*, my mother was glad, so I guess it's O.K."

"Hey, it's already summer, hasn't been much rain though, has there?"

"Yeah, Ryū, it's about that movie *Woodstock* but—did you see it?"

"Sure, why?"

"Don't you want to see it again, now? I wonder if it would be a letdown to see it now or not, what do you think?"

"Sure it'd be a letdown, but Jimi Hendrix would be great, he was really great."

"Yeah, it would be a letdown, wouldn't it? But maybe we'd feel something after all, but then afterwards it'd probably be a letdown, but I'd like to try and see it."

Yelling Yahyahyah, Tami and Bob flew past in a yellow sports car. Moko laughed, waved, and crushed out her cigarette with the slender high heel of her shoe.

"Have ya got any right to talk like that? What do ya mean to do, it's not just because we're not married or anything, what should Ah do, what do ya want? Ya want me to say Ah love ya? Is that it? Sure Ah'll say it, but just keep your hands off of me, and stop hassling me, Ah'm asking ya."

"Kei, it's not like that, don't get mad, it's not like that, what I'm saying is, you know, let's stop wearing each other out, right? We're just wearing each other out all the time, right? Let's stop, you know? You hear me, Kei?"

"Ah hear ya, hurry up, get it over with."

"I don't want to break up with you. I'll work on the docks, you know, in Yokohama I can get ¥6000 a day so it's really something, right? I can really make it and not use your bread anymore, I don't care if you mess around with other guys, I didn't say anything even about those black guys, right? Anyway let's just stop wearing each other out, it's just no good fighting like this, right? I'll go to work, tomorrow even, I'm real strong."

Kazuo's arm lay on Kei's shoulders. She didn't try to remove it. Right there in front of Yoshiyama, Kazuo crunched and swallowed two Nibrole pills and sneered at the two fighting.

Wearing just his pants, steam rising from his body, Okinawa sat on the kitchen floor and shot up with heroin.

Twisting her face, Reiko stuck the needle into the palm of her hand. Hey, Reiko, when did you learn to shoot up like that? Okinawa asked. Flustered, Reiko looked at me and winked. Why, Ryū showed me, of course.

"You're getting kind of stretched down there, Reiko."

"Don't talk funny. Me, I hate sex, don't you believe me? I don't have it with anybody but you."

Kei stood up, put on the Boz "First Album," and turned up the volume really high.

Yoshiyama said something but she pretended not to hear. He stretched out his hand to the amp to lower the sound and said, I've got something to talk over with you.

"There's nothing to talk over, Ah want to listen to Boz, hey, make it louder."

"Kei, that kiss mark on your neck's from Kazuo? Right? From Kazuo?"

"Ya idiot, it's from the party, one of the black guys. Look, see here? What a black guy did."

Kei rolled up her skirt and showed a big kiss mark on her thigh. Cut it out, Kei, Kazuo said. He pulled down her skirt.

"Yeah, I know about the one on your leg, but the one on your neck wasn't there yesterday, right? Hey, Ryū, it wasn't there, right? I guess you did it, Kazuo, it's O.K. if you did, but just say so, Kazuo.''

"My mouth isn't that big, is it? And if it's O.K., you don't have to make such a big thing of it, right?''

"Hey, Ryū, turn up the sound. Ever since Ah got up this morning Ah've been wanting to hear this, so that's why Ah came all the way over here, turn up the sound.''

I was lying on the bed and pretended not to hear Kei. It was too much trouble to get up and walk over to the amps. I trimmed my toenails. Reiko and Okinawa had spread out a blanket in the kitchen and were lying there on their stomachs.

"I'm not talking about any kiss mark or anything, I'm just saying what I always say. I'm saying something more—you know, basic. We should just be a little more, you know, better, you know, take care of each other, that's what I mean. We're living at kind of a different level from all the straights, so let's take care of each other.''

Rubbing his leg, Kazuo asked, "What's all that shit, Yoshi-yama? A different level from the straights? What're you talking about?''

Without looking at him, Yoshiyama said in a low voice, "None of your business.''

My toenails had a smell just like the pineapple. There was something poking my back; when I pulled aside the pillow and looked, it was the bra Moko had forgotten.

The wired bra was embroidered with flowers and smelled of detergent. I tossed it in the closet. The silver negligee was hanging there. I remembered the taste of Jackson's warm come and felt sick. I felt there must be a little bit left somewhere in my mouth; when I ran my tongue around, sometimes the taste seemed to come back. I tossed the nail parings on the veranda. I could see a woman walking a German shepherd in the garden of the hospital. She greeted someone passing her and stopped to talk. The dog pulled the chain taut. From where I was, the inside of the woman's mouth looked black, like back in the days when women used to dye their teeth, I thought her teeth must be really bad. She hid her mouth when she laughed. The dog strained forward and whined loudly.

"We, you know, we need each other. I mean, I don't know, but you're all I've got left, my mom's gone, and there're a lot of people against us, right? It'll be a bad scene if that welfare office guy finds you, and when they get me again this time it won't be just the juvie pen. We should help each other, just like we used to, remember how we swam in that river in Kyoto? I want things to be like they were back then, when we were just getting to know each other. I don't know why we have to fight like this, let's try and get along better, money's no problem, we've made out so far, and I'll go to work again. Hey, look, I'll go get a table and some shelves and stuff from that place Moko told us about in Roppongi, and there still seems to be a dresser and oven or something there, too. And then, Kei, you can paint them again.

"I'll get together some bread, right, I'll work, I'll get together some bread, and you can have another cat. Remember that gray Persian in the store, you said you want it? I'll buy it for you. And we'll find a new apartment, with its own john, and we'll get a new start.

"Yeah, we could even come here to Fussa like Ryū, get a house and have Reiko and Okinawa or somebody live in it with us, right? There're lots of rooms and lots of old GI houses around here, and we can get grass and have parties and stuff every day. A cheap used car even, Ryū has some foreigner friend who wants to sell one, we'll buy it and I'll get a driver's license. I can get one quick, and then we can go to the beach and stuff, right? And we'll have fun, Kei, we'll have fun.

"When my mom died, you know, I wasn't trying to put you

down, try and understand, it didn't mean she was more important than you, and anyway she's gone now, and you're all I've got left, right? Let's go home and start over.

"You see what I mean, Kei, you see what I mean?"

Yoshiyama lifted his hand to touch Kei's cheek. She brushed it away coldly, lowered her head, and laughed.

"So ya can really talk like that with a straight face, aren't ya ashamed? Everybody's listening, and what's that about your mom? That doesn't have anything to do with the way it is now, Ah don't know a thing about her, that time doesn't have a thing to do with it, Ah jes' don't like myself when Ah'm with ya, ya get me? Ah can't take it, Ah feel so small and lousy, when Ah'm with ya, Ah can't stand being so small and lousy."

Kazuo had been trying hard not to laugh out loud. As he listened to Yoshiyama, he'd clamped his hand over his own mouth, then when he heard Kei complaining again, his eyes met mine, and he couldn't hold it back any longer. "A Persian cat, how about that, that's rich!"

"Yoshiyama, ya hear me? If ya got something ya want to say, ya say it after ya get my necklace back from that pawnshop, O.K.? Say it after ya get back the gold necklace my papa gave me. Say it then.

"Ya're the one who pawned it, because ya said ya wanted to buy some Hyminal, ya got drunk and did it."

Kei started to cry. Her face fell apart. Kazuo finally stopped laughing.

"Hey, what're you talking about, Kei? You said I could pawn it, didn't you? You said you wanted to try Hyminal, you said it first, you said let's pawn it."

Kei wiped her tears. "Oh, stop it, ya're just that kind of guy, so it's no use. Ah guess ya didn't know, how Ah cried afterwards, ya didn't know how Ah cried on the way home. Ya were jes' singing, right?"

"What are you talking about? Don't cry, Kei, I'll get it out, I can get it out in no time. I'll work on the docks so I can get it out soon, it's not gone yet, don't cry, Kei."

As she blew her nose and wiped her eyes, Kei stopped responding to anything Yoshiyama said. Let's go out for a while, she said to Kazuo. Kazuo pointed to his leg and said, No, I'm tired, but she pulled him to his feet and when he saw the tears still in her eyes, he grudgingly agreed.

"Ryū, we'll be on the roof, so ya come up later and play the flute."

As the door closed, Yoshiyama called Kei's name loudly, but there was no answer.

Okinawa poured and brought in three cups of coffee. He was pale and shaky, and a little slopped on the rug.

"Hey, Yoshiyama, have some coffee, you're kind of hard to look at. Isn't it O.K.? No matter what, it doesn't mean a thing. Here . . . coffee."

Yoshiyama refused, Okinawa muttered So go to hell. Yoshiyama slouched over, stared at the wall, sighed from time to time, started to say something and then changed his mind. I could see Reiko lying on the kitchen floor. Her chest heaved slowly and her legs were thrown out wide like a dead dog's. Her body jerked now and then.

Yoshiyama ran his eyes over us, stood up, and started outside. He glanced down at Reiko, drank some water from the faucet, and opened the door.

Hey, Yoshiyama, don't go, stay here, I said. The only answer was the sound of the door closing.

Okinawa laughed bitterly and clicked his tongue.

"Nobody can do a thing about them, it's too late, but Yoshiyama's too dumb to know it. Ryū, you want to shoot up? This is awfully pure stuff, there's some left."

"No, that's O.K., I'm kind of dragged out today."

"Is that so? You're practicing your flute?"

"No."

"But you want to go on in music, right?"

"I haven't decided about that, you know, anyway I just don't want to do anything these days, don't feel like it."

Okinawa listened to The Doors' record he'd brought.

"So you're feeling let down?"

"Yeah, well, but it's different, kind of different from being let down."

"I met Kurokawa awhile back, he said he was really disgusted. He said he'd go to Algeria, be a guerrilla. Well, if he talked like that to somebody like me I guess he won't really go, but you're not thinking anything like that guy, huh?"

"Kurokawa? Yeah, it's different with me, I'm just, you know, my head's just all empty now, empty.

"A lot of things happened awhile back, right, but now I'm empty, can't do anything, you know? And because I'm empty I want to look around some more, I want to see lots of things."

The coffee was too strong to drink. I started boiling same more water to make it weaker.

"Well, so maybe you'll go to India."

"Huh? What about India?"

"You'd see a lot in India, I guess."

"Why would I have to go to India? That's not what I mean, there's plenty here. I'll look around here, I don't need to go somewhere like India."

"Well, you mean with Acid? You'll experiment with stuff like that? I don't get what you want to do."

"Yeah, I don't get it myself, I don't really know what I should do. But I'm not going to India or anything like that, nowhere I want to go, really. These days, you know, I look out the window, all by myself. Yeah, I look out a lot, the rain and the birds, you know, and the people just walking on the street. If you look a long time it's really interesting, that's what I mean by looking around. I don't know why, but these days things really look new to me.''

''Don't talk like an old man, Ryū, saying things look new is a sign of old age, you know.''

''No, it's different, that's not what I mean.''

''It's *not* different, you just don't know it because you're so much younger than me. Hey, you should play the flute, playing the flute's what you're supposed to do, try and do it right without running around with shit like Yoshiyama, hey, remember how you played on my birthday?

''It was over at Reiko's place, I really felt great then. That was when somehow my chest felt all crawly, like, I can't really say how I felt, but it was really good. I don't know how to say it but I felt, you know, like trying to make up with this guy I'd been fighting with. That's when I thought what a lucky guy you are, you know, I envied you, you could make people feel that way. I mean, I don't know, but because I can't do anything myself, I've never felt that way again—you can't know unless you really do it yourself. I'm nothing but a junkie, yeah, and when I run out of smack, there're times when I just can't stand it, wanting to shoot up, just wanting to shoot up, times when I'd kill someone if I could get it that way, but there's something I've thought about then. I've felt there was something, yeah, should be something between me and the smack. I mean, I'm shaking, rattling, I want to shoot up so bad I could go crazy, but I've felt just me and the White Lady aren't enough, somehow. When I finally do get to shoot up, I don't think about anything, but—it's not Reiko or my mom or anything, it's the flute you played that time. I thought I'd talk with you about it sometime. I don't know how you felt when you were playing, Ryū, but you know I felt really great? I'm always thinking I want something like you had then, I think about it when I'm sucking the smack up into the shooter. I'm finished, you know, because my body's already rotten. And look, my face, gone all flabby like this, I'm sure I'm going to kick off pretty soon now. I don't give a shit when I die, it doesn't matter, I'm not going to feel sorry about a thing.

"It's just, well, I'd like to know more about that feeling I had that time I heard your flute. That's all I feel, I want to know what that was. Maybe if I knew, I'd go off smack, well, maybe not. I'm not saying that's why you should, just you go play the flute, I'll sell some smack and buy you a good flute with the money."

Okinawa's eyes were bloodshot. He'd stained his pants with coffee as he talked.

"Hey, please, a Muramatsu would be great."

"Huh?

"A Muramatsu, you know, it's a kind of flute. I'd want a Muramatsu."

"A Muramatsu, huh? O.K. I'll get it for your birthday, and then you'll play for me again."

Hey, Ryū, you go and make him cut it out, I've had enough of both of them, I mean, my leg really hurts.

Breathing hard, Kazuo had opened the door and told us Yoshiyama was beating up Kei.

Okinawa lay flat on the bed.

From the direction of the roof we could clearly hear a scream. It sounded like Kei's. It wasn't the kind of voice you use to call someone, it was a real scream, the kind you can't hold back when you're being hit.

Kazuo sipped the cold coffee Yoshiyama had left, lit a cigarette, and started to change the bandage on his ankle. If you don't go quick, maybe Yoshiyama'll really kill her, he's really gone crazy, he muttered.

Okinawa sat up. "O.K., O.K., so let him, let them do what they want, I'm sick of them, absolutely. Hey, Kazuo, what happened to your leg?"

"Aw, I got bashed with a bat."

"Who did it?"

"A guard at Hibiya, you know, it's too much trouble to talk about, I shouldn't have gone."

"But it's a bruise, right? You don't need a bandage for a bruise, or did you break something?"

"Yeah, well, but this bat he had, nails sticking out of it, so I've got to keep it disinfected, right? Nail wounds, worst kind."

Beyond the washing fluttering in the wind, Yoshiyama was gripping Kei's hair and kicking her in the stomach. As his knee sank in, groans came from her swollen face.

She spat out blood and lay flat; I pulled Yoshiyama away from her. He was dripping cold sweat and the shoulder I touched had gone completely stiff.

On the bed Kei was groaning painfully, her teeth chattering, gripping the sheet and pressing the places where she'd been kicked. Reiko staggered from the kitchen and slapped the sobbing Yoshiyama on the cheek as hard as she could.

Making a face, Kazuo smeared a strong-smelling disinfectant on his own cuts. Okinawa melted a Nibrole pill in hot water and made Kei drink it.

That's real shit, kicking somebody in the belly! Yoshiyama, if Kei dies, you're a murderer, Okinawa said. Then I'll die, too, Yoshiyama sobbed. Kazuo sniggered.

Reiko put a cold towel on Kei's forehead and wiped the blood from her face. She checked Kei's stomach, saw the greenish bruises, and insisted she had to get to a hospital. Yoshiyama came over and peered into Kei's face, his tears dripping onto her stomach. Thick blood vessels beat in her temples, she kept spitting out yellow fluid. The lid, the white, even the iris of her right eye were completely red. Reiko opened Kei's cut lips and pressed in some gauze, trying to stop the blood flowing from a broken tooth.

Forgive me, forgive me, Kei, Yoshiyama said softly, his voice hoarse. Kazuo finished changing his own bandage and said, Forgive you, huh? So you've finally said it, that's too much.

"Go wash your face!"

Reiko gave Yoshiyama a shove and pointed toward the kitchen. "I can't stand looking at you like that anymore, so go on, wash your face."

Kei took her hand from her stomach and shook her head when Okinawa asked "Want me to shoot you up?" Moaning, she said, "Ah'm sorry, everybody, when ya were all feeling so good. But this is really the end of it, Ah'm really going to break it off now, that's why Ah put up with this."

"We weren't really feeling all that good, so don't worry about it, huh?" Okinawa grinned at her.

Yoshiyama started sobbing again.

"Kei, don't say you're going to break it off, Kei, don't leave me, please, forgive me, I'll do anything!"

Okinawa shoved him toward the kitchen.

"Look, we get the idea, so go wash your face."

Yoshiyama nodded and headed toward the kitchen, wiping his face on his sleeve. We could hear the sound of water.

When he came back into the room, Kazuo let out a yell. "This guy's had it," said Okinawa, shaking his head. Yoshiyama's left wrist was slashed open, his blood spattered on the rug. Reiko shrieked and closed her eyes. Kazuo jumped up and cried, "Ryū, call an ambulance!"

Holding the shaking arm above the wound with his other hand, Yoshiyama said through his nose, "Kei, you see what I mean?"

I started out to call an ambulance but Kei seized my arm and stopped me. She got up, supported by Reiko, and looked steadily into Yoshiyama's eyes. She went close to him and gently touched the wound. He'd stopped crying. She raised his split-open wrist and held it up before her eyes. She spoke with difficulty, twisting her swollen mouth.

"Yoshiyama, we're going out to eat now, nobody's had lunch yet so we're going out to eat. If ya want to die, ya go and die alone, right? So ya don't lay any hassle on Ryū, go outside and die alone."

A nurse carrying a bouquet passed along the wax-polished corridor. She had on only one sock; the other ankle was wrapped up in a yellow-splotched bandage. In front of me, a woman swinging her leg back and forth in boredom glanced at that big bouquet wrapped in glittering cellophane, tapped the shoulder of the woman next to her, who seemed to be her mother, and said in a whisper, "That must be expensive."

Hugging a number of weekly magazines with his left arm, a man with a crutch cut through the line of people waiting for medicine. From the thigh down his leg was stretched out stiffly, and white powder from the cast sprinkled out on his toes. Sticking out of that bent foot-shaped lump, the two smallest toes looked like no more than warts.

Next to me was an old man with layers of stiff bandage wrapped around his neck. The woman next to him was knitting.

"Well," he said, "I'm here to get my neck jerked around for me." White withered hairs straggled from his chin, and he watched the woman's regularly moving hands with slitlike eyes that were hard to tell from his wrinkles.

"And that really hurts, let me tell you, it hurts so much you'd rather die and you wonder why you don't. You get good and sick of it, you can be sure of that, I wonder if they can't do something else, what they do is just for old people."

Without resting her hands, the thick-necked dark woman looked at the old man, who put his hand on his neck and gave a wheezing laugh.

"My, that's just awful, isn't it?"

The old man's laugh turned into a hacking cough. He stroked his red- and brown-blotched face.

"Well, well, anyway old men shouldn't drive cars after all, my daughter-in-law said don't drive anymore, and she won't let me have the car anymore."

A cleaning woman in a white turban came along to wipe up the spots of Yoshiyama's blood from the floor.

The round-faced woman, bent over and carrying a mop and bucket, turned and called back loudly toward the end of the hall, "Kashi, Kashi, I'm O.K., just forget it."

At her voice, all the people sitting in the waiting room raised their heads. The woman began to mop, singing an old popular song.

"A suicide, is it? Well, since you're not dead it's just attempted suicide, but the fact is, you didn't do things right. Even cutting your wrist, well, human beings are pretty well put together, so as to keep on living. You'd have to press your wrist hard against a wall or something and pull up the skin to get the vein to stand out and then slash it. But if you were serious about it, if you really and truly want to die, you'd cut here, look here, under the ear, with a razor, and then even if an ambulance brought you to me right away there'd be no saving you."

That was what the doctor who fixed Yoshiyama's wrist had said. Yoshiyama had kept rubbing his eyes hard.

I thought he hadn't wanted this middle-aged doctor to know he was crying.

The old man with the bandaged neck spoke to the cleaning woman. "Does it clean up?"

"Huh? Well, if I get to it while it's still wet, yes, it cleans up pretty well, but you know how it is."

"That's awful, isn't it?"

"Huh, what's that?"

"I mean, it must be awful mopping up blood."

Children in wheelchairs were playing in the garden, throwing a yellow ball to each other. There were three of them, they all had very thin necks. When one of them missed, a nurse picked up the ball. As I looked closely I saw one boy had no hands; he joined in the game by batting the ball with his arms. Though the nurse threw the ball gently, it always veered off to one side when he hit it. He showed his teeth in laughter.

"I mean, I guess blood like that must be a bother. Well, I didn't go to the front lines in the war so I haven't seen much blood, and I was shocked to see it there, it's awful."

"I didn't go to the front lines either." The cleaning woman sprinkled white powder on the remaining blood. She got down on her knees and scrubbed with a brush.

The ball rolled into a puddle, and the nurse wiped it off with a towel. The child without hands, perhaps too excited to wait, shouted and waved his short arms.

"Hydrocholoric acid or something would clean it right up, wouldn't it?"

"That's for toilets. If you used it here, it'd ruin the whole floor."

The trees in the distance were shaking. The nurse went on tossing the ball to the children. A crowd of bulging pregnant women trooped off the bus and headed this way. A young man with a bouquet bounded up the stairs, and the woman who was knitting looked toward him. The cleaning woman hummed the same old song as before; the old man, whose neck wouldn't bend, was holding a newspaper up high to read it.

Yoshiyama's blood, mixed with the white powder, lay in pink bubbles on the floor.

"Ryu, I really was rotten, I-I'll get together some bread and go to India, work on the docks and get some bread, you know, I won't lay down any more hassles, I'm sorry, I'll go to India.''

Yoshiyama kept on talking like that on the way back from the hospital. There was blood on his rubber sandals and on his toes, and sometimes he touched his bandage. His face was still pale, but he said, It doesn't hurt. The pineapple I'd thrown away had rolled right beside the poplar tree. It was evening, no birds were in sight.

Kazuo wasn't in the room; Reiko said he'd gone home soon after everything happened.

''He should learn about guts from Yoshiyama, I wonder if he's kind of off somehow, he just doesn't understand anything,'' she said.

Okinawa shot up for the third time and rolled on the floor; the swelling on Kei's face had pretty well gone down. Yoshiyama sat in front of the TV.

''It's a movie about Van Gogh, Ryū, you should watch it.''

Reiko didn't answer when we asked for coffee. Yoshiyama told Kei he'd decided to go to India. Yeah, was all she said.

Reiko stood up and shook Okinawa's shoulder—he had a cigarette in his mouth and didn't budge—and she asked, Hey, where did you put what was left? When he said, Shit, it's all gone, that was the last, if you want some go buy it, she kicked his leg as hard as she could. Cigarette ashes spilled onto his naked chest. He laughed softly but didn't move, Reiko smashed his syringe on the concrete of the veranda.

''Hey, clean that up,'' I said.

Without answering she crunched and swallowed five Nibrole pills. Okinawa kept on laughing, his body shaking.

''Hey, Ryū, won't you play your flute some?'' he said, looking at me.

On the TV Kirk Douglas playing Van Gogh was shakily trying to cut off his ear.

Kei said, "Yoshiyama just copied this guy, everything ya do is jes' copying, right?"

Van Gogh let out a terrible yell and everyone except Okinawa turned toward the TV.

Stroking his bloody bandage, Yoshiyama spoke to Kei now and again. Is your stomach really O.K.? Today was really a breakthrough for me, and when I go to India, Kei, you can come with me as far as Singapore, and then I can see you off for Hawaii. Kei didn't say a word.

Okinawa's chest heaved slowly.

"Me," Reiko yelled suddenly, "I'm going to sell my body and buy smack, like Jackson told me! Ryū, take me to Jackson's house! He said I could come over anytime, I won't ask Okinawa anymore, take me to Jackson's place!"

Okinawa laughed again, his body shook.

"So go ahead and laugh, you damn junkie! Aren't you just a bum, in those lousy clothes, nothing but a bum? I'm sick of sucking your stinking limp prick! Me, I'm going to sell my bar, Ryū, and then I'll come out here and buy a car, buy smack, and then I'll go be Jackson's woman. Or Saburō would be O.K., too! I'll buy a camper, a bus I can live in, and have parties every day! Hey, Ryū, find that kind of bus for me.

"Okinawa, I guess you don't know what long pricks those blacks have. Even when they shoot up, they're still just as long, they go all the way into me. Hey, what have you got, you bum, do you know how much you stink?"

Okinawa got up and lit a cigarette. Without looking anywhere in particular he puffed the smoke out weakly.

"Reiko, you go back to Okinawa, I'll go along with you. That'd be the best thing, study at a beauty parlor again, I'll talk to your mother for you, this place is no good for you."

"Don't give me that, Okinawa, you just go back to sleep, next time even if you slash yourself up or you come crying and begging to me, I won't lend you any money, so *you* go back to Okinawa. You're the one who wants to go back, aren't you, but even if you want to, I won't give you the money to do it. Just try coming and crying to me when you're going cold turkey, just try crying and begging—lend me some bread, even a thousand yen'd be O.K.—I won't even give you one yen! You're the one who should go back to Okinawa!"

Okinawa lay down again and muttered, "So do what you want. Hey, Ryū, play the flute."

"I said I don't feel like it, didn't I?"

Yoshiyama silently watched the TV.

Kei, still seeming to be in some pain, crunched a Nibrole. There was the sound of a pistol shot, Van Gogh's neck twisted, and Yoshiyama muttered, Aw, he got it.

There was a moth on the pillar.

At first I thought it was just a spot, but as I stared at it, it changed its position slightly. There was a faint down on the ash-gray wings.

After everyone had left, the room seemed darker than usual. It wasn't that the light was weaker . . . I seemed to have moved far away from the source of light.

A lot of stuff had fallen on the floor. That rolled-up ball of hair must be Moko's. The wrapping paper from a cake Lilly had bought, bread crumbs, red and black and translucent nail parings, flower petals, dirty tissue paper, women's underwear, Yoshi-yama's dried blood, socks, stubbed-out cigarettes, glass, bits of aluminum foil, a mayonnaise bottle.

Record jackets, film, a star-shaped candy box, a syringe case, a book—the book was a collection of Mallarmé's poetry that Kazuo had forgotten. On the back cover of Mallarmé I squashed the belly of a moth with black and white stripes. There seemed to be a little cry, different from the sound of the fluid bursting from its swollen belly.

"Ryū, you're tired, your eyes look funny, shouldn't you go home and get some sleep?"

After I'd killed the moth, I'd felt strangely hungry. I'd gnawed on some leftover roast chicken from the refrigerator. But it had gone completely bad; its sour taste stabbed my tongue and spread through my head. When I'd tried to pull out the sticky lump stuck in the back of my throat, a chill wrapped my whole body. It was intense and sudden, as if I'd been beaten. No matter how much I rubbed at my gooseflesh, it stayed on the back of my neck, no matter how often I rinsed my mouth, I could still taste the sourness and my gums felt slimy. The chicken skin caught between my teeth numbed my tongue. The piece of chicken I'd spit out, wet with saliva, floated soggily in the sink. A small cube of potato blocked the drain, and grease made rings on the surface of the dirty water. When I seized the cube between my fingernails and pulled it out, trailing strings of slime, the water began to go down, the piece of chicken moved in a circle and was sucked into the hole.

"Shouldn't you go home and get some sleep? Have all those weirdos left your place?"

Lilly was straightening her bed. I could see her buttocks swelling under her translucent negligee. In the red light from the ceiling, the ring on her left hand sparkled, a light of the same size glinting in its facets.

The big lump of roast chicken had caught in the drain. With a sucking sound it stuck to the four small holes there. On the sticky lump, even though it had been gnawed by my teeth and partly dissolved by saliva, I could still see the feather holes clearly, and some bristles like plastic. A smelly grease clung to my hands, the smell didn't come off even when I washed them. Then when I went back from the kitchen into the living room, while I was walking over to get a cigarette from on top of the TV, I was seized with an indescribable uneasiness. It was as if I'd been embraced by an old woman with skin disease.

"Have all those weirdos left your place? Ryū, I'll make some coffee for you."

The round white table Lilly was always so proud of, made by convicts in Finland, reflected the light. I could just make out a faint green tint on its surface. Once I'd noticed it, that special green grew stronger in my eyes; it was like the faint green next to the orange trembling on the sea at sunset.

"Why don't you drink some coffee? I'll even put in some brandy, you need a good sleep. I've been feeling kind of funny, too, since that night, I haven't been going to work. And I've got to get the car fixed, it's terribly scratched up, you know, it didn't get dented but the cost of painting's so high these days, I really don't know what I'll do. But I'd like to try it once more, you know, Ryū."

Lilly stood up from the sofa. Her voice was muffled. I felt like I was seeing an old movie, like Lilly was far off and sending her voice through a long tube. I felt that what was here now was an elaborate Lilly-doll. It moved just its mouth, and a tape recording made long ago was being played.

No matter what I'd done, I couldn't get rid of the cold that had wrapped my body back in my own room. When I took out a sweater and put it on, when I closed the veranda doors and pulled the curtains, I began to sweat, but even then the chill was still there all the time.

The sound of the wind in the closed room became faint, it only sounded like a ringing in my ears. Not being able to see outside gave me the feeling of being trapped.

I hadn't much noticed what was outside before, but just as if I'd been staring at the scene for a long time, the drunk crossing the street, the red-haired girl running, the empty can thrown from a passing car, the poplars stretching up blackly, the bulk of the hospital at night and the stars all floated before my eyes with a mysterious clarity. And at the same time, shut away from the world outside, I felt cut off and thrown away. The room was filled with unusual vapors; I had trouble breathing. Cigarette smoke rose and from somewhere came the smell of melting butter.

As I looked for the place where that smell leaked in, I stepped on some dead insects, and their juices and dusty scales dirtied my toes. I heard a dog howl; when I turned on the radio, there was the Van Morrison song "Domino." When I turned on the TV, there was suddenly a close-up of a raging shaven-headed man yelling, "Isn't that just what anyone would expect!" When I turned it off, the screen darkened as if it had been sucked up and my own distorted face appeared. My image on the dark screen, flapping its lips, saying something to itself.

"Ryū, I found a novel with someone just like you in it, really like you."

Lilly sat on a chair in the kitchen, waiting for the water to boil in a round glass perculator. She batted at a small flying insect. I sank down into the sofa where Lilly's body had been and ran my tongue over my lips again and again.

"Well, this guy has some whores working for him in Las Vegas and so he gets women for parties for a lot of rich people—isn't that like you, Ryū? But he's still young—I thought that's like you, too. You're nineteen?"

The surface of the glass clouded whitely and steam began to rise. The trembling flame of the alcohol lamp was reflected on the window. Lilly's huge shadow moved on the wall. Small dense shadows from the electric bulb on the ceiling and large faint shadows from the alcohol lamp overlapped and the overlappings moved complexly, like living things, just like amoebas dividing and redividing.

"Ryū, are you listening?"

Uh-huh, I answered. My voice, stopping on my hot dry tongue, seemed to come out like the voice of a completely different person. Feeling uneasily that perhaps it wasn't my own voice, I was afraid to talk. Toying with a feathered hat, sometimes opening her negligee to scratch her chest, Lilly said, "And this guy, you know, he makes a whore out of this girl who was his best friend back in high school."

Okinawa, the last to leave, had put on his smelly work clothes and closed the door behind him without saying good-bye.

"And this guy is the bastard kid of some whore, too, but his father was the crown prince of some little country, he's the kid left by this crown prince who came to Las Vegas in disguise to have some fun."

What could Lilly be talking about?

My sight wasn't normal. Everything I saw was strangely misty. It was as if the slime in the milk bottle on the table beside Lilly were spreading. The stuff was even on her as she bent forward. Rather than just being on the surface, the stuff seemed to have appeared after the skin was peeled off.

I remembered a friend who'd died of a bad liver, and what he'd always said. Yeah, he'd said, maybe it's just my idea, but really it always hurts, the times it don't hurt is when we just forget, we just forget it hurts, you know, it's not just because my belly's all rotten, everybody always hurts. So when it really starts stabbing me, somehow I feel sort of peaceful, like I'm myself again. It's hard to take, sure, but I feel sort of peaceful. Because it's always hurt ever since I was born.

"This guy goes to the desert, at dawn, flying along in his car he goes into the Nevada desert."

Into the bubbling, boiling glass sphere, Lilly spooned black powder from a brown can. The smell drifted to me. When Jackson and Rudianna had straddled me, I really thought of myself as a yellow doll. How had I become a doll then?

Now, bent over, her red hair dangling down her back, Lilly looked like a doll. An old, moldly smelling doll, a doll that says the same words over and over when you pull a string, and when you pry open a lid in its chest there'd be some silver batteries, a doll made so that its eyes flash when it talks. The crisp red hairs had been inserted one by one, if you put milk in its mouth, the sticky fluid would drip out a hole in its bottom. Even if you banged it hard on the floor, as long as the tape recorder inside wasn't broken the doll would go on talking. Ryū, good morning, I'm Lilly, Ryū, how are you? I'm Lilly, good morning, Ryū, how are you? I'm Lilly, good morning.

"And this guy, in the Nevada desert, he sees where the H-bombs are kept. H-bombs as big as buildings all lined up, on a base at dawn."

Back there in my room the cold all around me had slowly gotten worse. I'd put on more clothes, crawled under the blankets, drank whiskey, opened and closed the door and tried to sleep. I drank strong coffee, did some exercises, smoked I don't know how many cigarettes. I read a book, turned off all the lights and turned them on again. I opened my eyes and stared for a long time at the spots on the ceiling, then closed my eyes and counted them. I remembered the plots of movies I'd seen long ago, and Male's missing tooth, Jackson's prick, Okinawa's eyes, Moko's butt, Rudianna's pubic hair.

On the other side of the closed veranda doors several drunks passed, loudly singing an old song. I thought it was like a chorus of prisoners in chains, or a war song sung together by badly wounded shell-shocked Japanese soldiers before they threw themselves off a cliff. Turned toward the dark sea, bandages on their faces, holes oozing pus or with maggots crawling on their thin bodies, Japanese soldiers bowing to the East without any light in their eyes—it sounded like a sad song they would sing.

As I listened to the song and gazed vacantly at my distorted self reflected on the TV, I felt sunk in a deep dream from which I couldn't rise no matter how I struggled. My self reflected on the TV and the Japanese soldiers singing behind my eyes overlapped. And the black dots making those overlapping images, the black dots clustering to make the images float up, crawled in swarms inside my head just like the numberless caterpillars that thrive and squirm on peach trees. The ragged black dots rustled and formed an unnerving shape without a shape, and I realized I was covered with gooseflesh. My muddy eyes on the dark screen buckled as if melting, and I muttered to that self, who *are* you?

What are you afraid of, I'd said.

"These missiles, hey, you know, these ICBMs, they were all lined up in that wide empty Nevada desert. On the desert where people look just like bugs. These missiles were there, missiles just like buildings."

The inside of the glass sphere was boiling. The black fluid bubbled, Lilly slapped a flying insect. She peeled off the dead insect that become a single line on her palm and threw it in the ashtray. Purple smoke rose from the ashtray. It mingled with the steam rising from the black liquid. Lilly's slim fingers held a cigarette, she covered the alcohol lamp to put it out. The huge shadow on the wall spread throughout the entire room for a moment and then faded. The shadow disappeared just like a ballon pricked with a pin. It was sucked up by the smaller, denser shadows made by the light bulb on the ceiling.

Lilly handed me a cup of coffee.

When I looked in, my reflection trembled on the surface.

"And when this guy, he yells at the missiles from the top of the hill, a lot had happened to him and he didn't understand why. he didn't understand what he'd been doing up until then, or who he was then, or what he should do from then on, and he didn't have anyone to talk to, and he was just feeling fed up and all alone. So he turned toward the missiles and yelled in his head Blow up! Go on and blow up for me!"

I noticed a growth on the surface of the black liquid. When I was in grade school, my grandmother had gone into the hospital with cancer.

She'd had an allergy to the pain-killer the doctor gave her, and her whole body had broken out in a rash and the rash had changed the shape of her face. When I went to see her, she'd said, clawing at the rash, Little Ryū, your granny's going to die, I have this thing and it's going to take me to the next world, your granny's going to die. Something just like that rash on my grandmother was floating on the surface of the black liquid. At Lilly's urging I drank. When the hot liquid entered my throat, I felt the cold already there inside of me mix with the growth on the surface of things.

"Ryū, isn't that like you somehow, that's what I thought, when I first started reading, I thought it was like you."

Lilly talked while sitting on the sofa. Her leg made an odd curve and was swallowed up in a red slipper. Once when I'd dropped Acid in a park, I'd felt the same way I did now. I could see the trees stretching up to the night sky and some foreign town between the trees, and I walked there. In that dream town nobody passed me, the doors were all closed; I walked alone. When I walked to the outskirts of the town an emaciated man stopped me and told me to go no further. When I went on anyway, my body began to grow cold, and I thought I was dead. Face pale, my dead self sat down on a bench and began to turn toward my real self, who was watching this hallucination on the screen of the night. My dead self came nearer, just as if it might want to shake hands with my real self. That's when I panicked and tried to run. But my dead self pursued me and finally caught me, entered me and controlled me. I'd felt then just the way I felt now. I felt as if a hole had opened in my head from which consciousness and memory leaked out and in their place the rash crowded in, and a cold like spoiled roast chicken. But that time before, shaking and clinging to the damp bench, I'd told myself, Hey, take a good look, isn't the world still under your feet? I'm on this ground, and on this same ground are trees and grass and ants carrying sand to their nests, little girls chasing rolling balls, and puppies running.

This ground runs under countless houses and mountains and rivers and seas, under everywhere. And I'm on it.

Don't be scared, I'd told myself, the world is still under me.

"I thought about you, Ryū, as I read that novel. I wondered what you're going to do from now on, I don't know about this guy in the book—haven't finished reading it yet."

When I was a child, whenever I used to run and fall, I'd get stinging scrapes, and I liked to have them painted with a piercing, strong-smelling medicine. On the bloody scraped place something was always stuck, earth or mud or grass juice or crushed insects, and I liked the pain of the medicine as it soaked in with its bubbles. My play over, watching the sun go down, I'd frown and blow on the wound, and then I felt a sense of peace, as if I and the gray evening landscape were confiding in each other. Just the opposite from heroin or melting together in a woman's juices, the pain made me stand out from my surroundings, the pain made me feel as if I were shining. And I thought this shining self could get along well with the lovely orange light of the setting sun. Back in my room, as I'd remembered this, I'd tried to do something about the unbearable cold, and I'd put in my mouth the wing of a dead moth that had been lying on the rug. The moth had stiffened, green fluid had come from its belly and hardened slightly. The gold scale-dust shone on my finger, the little black spheres, the eyes, drew threads after them when they separated from the body. When I broke the wing and put it on my tongue, its fine hairs stabbed my gums.

"Is the coffee good? Say something, Ryū, Ryū, what's the matter? What are you thinking about?"

Lilly's body, made of metal. If the white skin were peeled off, a sparkling alloy might appear.

Yeah, uh-huh, it's good, Lilly, good, I answered. My left hand twitched. I took a deep breath. On the wall was a poster—a little girl, who'd cut her foot on glass while jumping rope in a vacant lot. There was a strange smell around. I dropped the cup of hot black fluid.

What are you doing, Ryū? What's the matter with you, anyway?

Lilly came over, holding a white cloth. The white cup had broken, and the carpet sucked up the fluid. Vapor rose. The liquid became lukewarm and sticky between my toes.

You're shaking? What is it, what's the matter? I touched Lilly's body. It seemed hard and rough like stale bread. Her hand was on my knee. Go wash your feet, the shower's still working, go wash them, quick. Lilly's face was twisted. She bent over to pick up the broken pieces of the cup. She put them on the smiling face of a foreign girl on the cover of a magazine. Some coffee was left in one of the pieces, and she poured it into the ashtray. A smoldering cigarette hissed as it went out. Lilly noticed that I'd stood up. Her face shone with beauty cream. I thought something was funny from the beginning, she said, what is it with you? Anyway go wash your feet, I won't have you staining the rug. Drawn by the sofa, I started walking. My forehead was hot and I felt dizzy from the spinning and tilting of the room. Go wash quick, what are you staring at? Go wash up.

The tiles of the shower stall were cold and the dangling hose reminded me of a death chamber with an electric chair I'd seen in a photo sometime. There was red-stained underwear on the washing machine, a spider ran around drawing a thread along the yellow tile wall. Without making any noise I ran the water over the soles of my feet. The netlike cover of the drain was blocked by a piece of paper. As I'd come here from my place, I'd passed through the hospital garden, where the lights were out. Then, aiming at a bush, I'd thrown away the body of the moth I'd been holding tightly. The morning sun would dry up the fluids, and maybe some starving insects would feed on it, I thought.

What are you doing? Hey, Ryū, go home, I can't get along with you. Lilly looked at me. Leaning on the door post, she tossed the white cloth she held into the shower stall. It was a little stained by black fluid. Like a newborn baby opening its eyes for the first time, I stared at Lilly in her whitely shining negligee. What's that fluffy stuff, what are those turning, shining balls under it, and the bulge with two holes under that, what is that black hole enclosed by those two soft pieces of flesh, what are the little white bones inside, what is it—that moist red thin piece of flesh?

There was the sofa with its pattern of red flowers, the gray walls, the hairbrushes with red hairs caught on them, the pink rug, the spotted cream-colored ceiling with dry flowers hanging from it, the cloth cord wound around an electric wire that hung straight down, the trembling flashing light bulb under that twisted cord, and a thing like a crystal tower inside the bulb. The tower whirled at a tremendous speed, my eyes hurt as if burned, when I closed them I saw the laughing faces of scores of people and I had trouble breathing. Hey, tell me what's wrong, you're so jittery, are you going crazy? The red afterimage of the light bulb spilled over Lilly's face. The afterimage spread and warped and broke like melting glass, and scattered into spots across my entire field of vision. Lilly's red-spotted face came close and she touched my cheek.

Hey, why are you shaking? Say something.

I remembered a man's face, his face had spots, too. It was the face of an American medic who'd rented a house of my aunt's in the country. Ryū, you're all covered with goose bumps, really, what's the matter? Say something, I'm scared.

When I'd gone to collect the rent for my aunt, the medic had always let me see the hairy crotch of a thin monkey-faced Japanese woman there. I'm O.K., Lilly, yeah, O.K., it's nothing. I just can't calm down, it's always like this after a party.

In the medic's room, in that room decorated with New Guinean spears, their tips smeared with poison, he'd showed me the crotch of that heavily madeup woman, her legs beat the air.

You're stoned, aren't you? Is that it?

I felt I was being sucked into Lilly's eyes, that she was swallowing me up.

The medic had opened the woman's mouth for me. Her teeth melted, he'd said in Japanese and laughed. Lilly took out some brandy. You're not O.K. Should I take you to the hospital? The woman, her mouth opened wide like a hole, had screeched. Lilly, I don't know what's the matter, maybe if you have some Philopon you could shoot me up, I want to calm down.

Lilly tried to force me to drink some brandy. I bit hard on the rim of the glass, seeing the ceiling light through the moist glass, spots overlapping spots, my dizziness got worse and I felt nauseated. There's none left, Ryū, because after that mesc I shot it all up, I felt really nervous and shot it all up.

The medic had stuck various things up the thin woman's butt and showed me. The woman had rubbed her lipstick on the sheets, panted, glared at me, turned toward the whiskey-drinking laughing medic and screeched Gimme ciggy. Lilly made me sit down on the sofa. Lilly, I really haven't been taking anything, it's different from that time, it's completely different from that time with the jet.

That time, you know, I was all full of the smell of the fuel oil, that time was scary, too, but this time's different, I'm empty, there's nothing. My head's so hot I can't stand it but I'm cold, I can't get rid of the cold. And I can't make myself do what I want very well, it's weird even talking like this, just like I'm talking in a dream.

Like I'm talking in a scary dream I can't get out of, it's scary. Even when I've been talking like this I've been thinking about something entirely different, about an idiot Japanese woman, not you Lilly, someone else. I've had that woman and a GI medic in my mind all the time. But I really know I'm not dreaming. I know my eyes are open and I'm here, that's why it's scary. I'm so scared I almost want to die, want you to kill me. Yeah, I really want you to kill me, I'm scared just standing here.

Lilly pushed the brandy glass between my teeth again. The warm liquid shook my tongue and slid down my throat. The ringing in my ears filled my whole head. The veins in my palms stood out, their color was gray, they pulsed grayly. Sweat ran down my neck, and Lilly wiped the cold sweat for me. You're just tired, you'll be O.K. after a good night's sleep.

Lilly, maybe I should go back, I want to go back. I don't know where but I want to go back there, I must have got lost. I want to go to someplace cooler, I used to be there, I want to go back. You know it, too, Lilly? A place like under big trees that smell real good—where am I now? Where am I?

The back of my throat seemed dry enough to burst into flame. Lilly shook her head, drank the rest of the brandy herself, and muttered This is a bad scene. I remembered that guy Green Eyes. Have you seen the black bird? You'll be able to see the black bird, Green Eyes had told me. Outside this room, beyond that window, a huge black bird might be flying. A bird as huge as the black night itself, a black bird dancing in the sky just like the gray birds I always saw pecking crumbs, but just because it was so huge all I could see of it was the hole in its beak like a cave beyond the window, I guess I couldn't ever see the whole of it. The moth I'd killed must have died without seeing the whole of me.

It was just that something huge had crushed that soft belly full of green fluids, and the moth died without knowing that was part of me. Now I was just like the moth, going to be crushed by the black bird. I guess Green Eyes had come to tell me that, he'd tried to tell me.

Lilly, can you see the bird? There's a bird flying outside now, right? Don't you see it? I know, the moth didn't know, but I know. The bird, the big black bird—Lilly, you know it, too?

Ryū, you're going crazy, pull yourself together! Don't you understand? You're going crazy!

Lilly, don't kid me, I know. I won't be fooled, not anymore, I know, I know where I am. This is the place nearest the bird, I've got to be able to see it from here.

I know, I've really known for a long time, finally I understand, it's been the bird. I've lived till now so I could understand this.

It's the bird, Lilly, can you see it?

Stop it! Stop it, Ryū, stop it!

Lilly, do you know where this is? I wonder how I got here. The bird's flying just like it should, look, it's flying there beyond the window, the bird that's destroyed my city.

Sobbing, Lilly slapped my cheek.

Ryū, you're going crazy, don't you understand?

I guess Lilly couldn't see the bird, she opened the window. Sobbing, she threw open the window, the nighttime town spread out below us. Tell me where your bird's flying, take a good look, there's no bird anywhere!

I smashed the brandy glass on the floor. Lilly shrieked. The glass flew apart. The pieces glittered on the floor.

Lilly, that's the bird, look hard, that town is the bird, that's not a town or anything, there're no people or anything living in it, that's the bird, don't you see? Don't you really see? When that guy yelled at the missiles to blow up in the desert, he was trying to kill the bird. We've got to kill the bird, if it's not killed I won't understand about myself anymore, the bird's in the way, it's hiding what I want to see. I'll kill the bird, Lilly, if I don't kill it I'll be killed. Lilly, where are you, come and kill the bird with me, Lilly, I can't see anything, Lilly, I can't see a thing.

I rolled on the floor. Lilly ran outside.

There was the sound of a car starting up.

The light bulb spun. The bird was flying, flying outside the window. Lilly was gone, the huge black bird was coming here. I picked up a fragment of glass from the rug, gripped it, and jabbed it into my shaking arm.

The sky was cloudy, it wrapped me and the sleeping hospital like a soft white cloth. As the wind cooled my still burning cheeks there was the sound of leaves rubbing together. The wind held dampness, the smell of plants at night, it brought the smell of plants breathing quietly at night. In the hospital, there were red emergency lights only in the entranceway and lobby, the rest was dark. The many windows, marked off by narrow aluminum frames, reflected the sky waiting for dawn.

That twisting purple line must be a crack in the clouds, I thought.

Now and then passing headlights lit up the bushes shaped like children's caps. The moths that had been thrown out didn't reach this far. On the ground were little stones mixed with bits of dried grass. When I tried picking some up, I saw the morning dew had soaked the down covering it—just like dead insects covered with cold sweat.

Back then, when I'd run out of Lilly's room, I'd felt my bloody left arm to be the only living part of me. I put the thin fragment of glass, dripping blood, in my pocket, and ran out into the misty road. The doors and windows of the houses were shut, nothing was moving. I thought I'd been swallowed by a huge living thing, that I was turning around and around in its stomach like the hero of some fairy tale.

I fell again and again, so that the glass in my pocket broke into little pieces.

As I was crossing an empty space, I collapsed on the grass. I bit the damp grass blades. Their bitterness pricked my tongue and a little bug resting on the grass ended up in my mouth.

The bug wriggled around with its scratchy little legs.

I put my finger in and the round bug with a pattern on its back crawled out, wet with my saliva. Sliding on its wet legs, it returned to the grass. As I felt the places on my gums the bug had scratched with my tongue, the dew on the grass cooled my body. The smell of grass surrounded me, and I felt the fever that had racked my body slowly escape into the ground.

All the time I was being touched by something I didn't understand, I thought as I lay on the grass. Surely even now, even in the garden of this gentle nighttime hospital, that hadn't changed. The huge black bird was flying even now, and I and the bitter grass and the round bug were all shut up together in its womb.

Unless my body dried up hard like moths that became like pebbles, I couldn't escape from the bird.

I took a fragment of glass about the size of my thumbnail out of my pocket and wiped the blood off it. The little fragment with its smooth hollow reflected the brightening sky. Under the sky stretched the hospital and far away the tree-lined street and the town. The horizon of the shadowy reflected town made a delicate curving line. Its curves were the same, the same as the time I'd almost killed Lilly on the runway in the rain, that white curved line that burned for an instant with the thunder. Like the wave-filled foggy horizon of the sea, like a woman's white arm, a gentle curve.

All the time, since I didn't know when, I'd been surrounded by this whitish curving.

The fragment of glass with the blood on its edge, as it soaked up the dawn air, was almost transparent.

It was a boundless blue, almost transparent. I stood up, and as I walked toward my own apartment, I thought, I want to become like this glass. And then I want to reflect this smooth white curving myself. I want to show other people these splendid curves reflected in me.

The edge of the sky blurred with light, and the fragment of glass soon clouded over. When I heard the songs of birds, there was nothing reflected in the glass, nothing at all.

Beside the poplar in front of the apartment lay the pineapple I'd thrown out yesterday. From its moist cut end there still drifted the same smell.

I crouched down on the ground and waited for the birds.

If the birds dance down and the warm light reaches here, I guess my long shadow will stretch over the gray birds and the pineapple and cover them.

Letter to Lilly

Lilly, where are you now? I think it was four years ago, I tried going to your house once more, but you weren't there. If you read this book, get in touch with me.

I had just one letter from Augusta, who went back to Louisiana. She says she's driving a taxi. She told me to say Hi to you. Maybe you even married that half-Japanese painter. But I don't care, even if you're married, I think I'd like to see you just once more if I can. Just once more, I want the two of us to sing ''Que sera sera'' again.

And just because I've written this book, don't think I've changed. I'm like I was back then, really.

Ryū

（新装版）英文版 限りなく透明に近いブルー
Almost Transparent Blue

2003 年 2 月　第 1 刷発行
2006 年 8 月　第 5 刷発行

著　者　　　村上　龍

訳　者　　　ナンシー・アンドリュー

発行者　　　冨田　充

発行所　　　講談社インターナショナル株式会社
　　　　　　〒112-8652　東京都文京区音羽 1-17-14
　　　　　　電話　03-3944-6493（編集部）
　　　　　　　　　03-3944-6492（マーケティング部・業務部）
　　　　　　ホームページ　www.kodansha-intl.com

印刷・製本所　大日本印刷株式会社

落丁本、乱丁本は購入書店名を明記のうえ、講談社インターナショナル業務部宛
にお送りください。送料小社負担にてお取替えいたします。なお、この本につい
てのお問い合わせは、編集部宛にお願いいたします。本書の無断複写（コピー）
は著作権法上での例外を除き、禁じられています。

定価はカバーに表示してあります。

© 村上龍 1976
Printed in Japan
ISBN4-7700-2904-7